The Twelve Days of Christmas

By Rebecca Bonnington

Day One - The Therapist

14th December

Her office was a neat and tidy place. It was comfortable with just enough cushions to look welcoming and not so many that it looked like an interior designer's show room. It had plenty of natural light, which Rachel liked because it was often the light coming in through the large plain glass windows that distracted her clients from their troubles.

Rachel hadn't given her workspace a name. The only one she could think of at the time she set it up was The Sanctuary and it sounded too twee. Besides, she'd once seen some bath salts in Boots that had The Sanctuary neatly embossed in gold lettering on an orange label and she certainly hadn't wanted people to think she offered spa treatments in her office.

When Rachel spoke to her prospective clients, she directed them to her home address and then asked them to text her when they arrived, that way she could slip on her expensive sheepskin slippers off and pop her garden shoes on, taking the twenty metre walk through the large, expertly landscaped garden into the house, complete with its' Aga, granite work surfaces and kitchen island unit to the front door where she greeted them with a warm smile and a handshake.

There was usually some lightweight chat about finding the house successfully, the weather and there being no need to remove their shoes when they came in. Rachel was good at keeping the conversation light, aware that her clients were often nervous when they first arrived. Walking along the gravel path, brushing past the sweet-smelling lilac in the summer, the dark brown stalks of last year's flowers in the winter would also help to calm any nerves.

If was raining, they would have to rush, shoulders hunched against the wet, heads bowed, the distance too short to warrant an umbrella. There was an umbrella at the back door to avoid getting completely drenched when downpours were torrential, but mostly her clients took the time to observe their green surroundings before unburdening themselves in Rachel's haven.

Rachel thought there was something about taking steps through the greenery passing the plants and flowers in various states of bloom or decay that allowed her clients space to believe that everything will be alright in the end. Nature has a great way of healing without intervention from other humans. She often wondered whether sending her clients on a gardening course or trekking in the mountains would do just as much good as the kind of talking therapy she practiced.

People found Rachel when they needed her. It's something she tried to analyse in a vain attempt to create a marketing strategy in the beginning. She quickly gave this up realising that people responded to their own needs and not her desire to make money. There's the ubiquitous website which some people read and some didn't. It often amazed her how many people sought her out without knowing much about her. She thought that probably said more about their desperation than her expertise.

Rachel gets the people who have tried everything. They've come to the end of the line with traditional therapies, with their Dr and with their friends and family. Sometimes, they came to her because of their friends, but usually it's because of their families.

The poet, W H Auden was right, your parents do definitely fuck you up and if they don't, then some teacher, boss, boyfriend, girlfriend or occasionally random stranger does it instead. If we all live in neat, tidy little bubbles which had a thick layer called defence against emotional crap covering it, society wouldn't need people like Rachel.

Perhaps Rachel understood this more than most people. Her life had not gone to plan. Yes, she'd got married, had a daughter and then a son, bought a large house in the country and got ready to settle into a routine of school runs, work, holidays and dinner parties with well-chosen friends from suitable backgrounds. Despite her efforts, the middle class idyll of married life had eluded her and she'd found herself at the sharp end of a toxic relationship which ended in the worst way possible. Neither her or her ex-husband came out of it covered in glory. Rachel didn't like to dwell on the final chapter of that relationship, it had left an indelible stain on her which she hoped no one could see.

Joyce came to Rachel's door on one particular December day. She didn't look like her usual client. Rachel was an expensive person to visit and her clients were normally middle to upper class professionals with plenty of cash. Joyce's appearance was almost smart, it was clean and neat, but her high street coat was worn thin around the collar and had the look of having been cleaned several times too many.

Her hair was badly cut, cropped closely and unflatteringly against her thin head. The grey showed at the roots giving her a distinctly old look, something that the hair dye was attempting to cover up and failing miserably to do so.

Then there was her smell. Deep fat fryers. No matter how hard you might try, removing the smell of years of deep fat frying cannot be masked with mid-priced perfume. Joyce would have had to have spent all her money on high end candles and defusers for the next five years to get rid of that particular stale smell of impoverishment from her home, let alone her clothes.

Joyce sat herself down uncomfortably adjusting her skirt and pulling at the collar of her pale blue blouse. Rachel hung her coat up for her on the professional trendy-looking coat stand which had come from John Lewis' sale several years ago. Joyce's aged coat looked very much at odds with the pale beech curves of the Scandinavian design-inspired piece of furniture it hung on. She wrung her hands over and over again, twisted the band on her ring finger of her left hand and constantly looked down. She found it almost impossible to make eye contact. Rachel was curious to know what Joyce was going to reveal.

She began as she always did, "So, Joyce, tell me what you need today."

This question brought a mixed response from Rachel's clients. Some of them claimed they had no idea why they'd come and some dived straight into long explanations as to precisely why they needed Rachel to help them. Joyce did neither. She didn't speak.

"Can I get you a tea, coffee or water Joyce?"

Breaking her current state of mind with something innocuous had felt like the right thing to do.

"Water. Please," she replied, her stare fixed intently on her writhing hands, as though the answer to her issues were stored in there.

Rachel got up from her usual seat and walked slowly over to the tiny sink in the corner of the garden room office. Her movements were slow during those days as the baby she was carrying was due in four weeks' time. She had the usual paraphernalia for tea and coffee making with the recent addition of an automatic coffee making machine. One of the ones that looks very pleased with itself and is advertised by film stars which requires no more than an expensive capsule to make the drink. She didn't use it that often, but her clients seemed to approve.

She handed the cold glass of water to Joyce who took it without looking up.

"If it's easier for you Joyce, you can write down your reasons for coming to see me." This was usually her last resort as she didn't like her clients to commit their darkest thoughts to paper, she liked them to think about the possibilities of change for the future and not the hurt or trauma of their past.

"Keep your writing short Joyce and just tell me what you want for your life. We can explore things in more detail once you've got what you want out in the open." Her voice was always kind, soft, but with an edge of firmness which she thought gave her clients a sense of safety. Her two children called it her work voice and had knew that it meant she wanted them to do something that they were unlikely to want to do.

"No one has ever asked me what I want before," Joyce's voice was timid and she just about managed to look at Rachel when she spoke. Her speech was articulate, intelligent, giving no signal that her social status was as low as her clothes suggested.

"It's funny, a few people say that to me when they first see me. It's okay to want things and it's okay to tell me what you want, so please, go ahead. I'll listen and ask questions if I need to and only interrupt if I hear you're going round in circles or down a rabbit hole that doesn't appear to serve you well." Rachel left a silence that she expected Joyce to fill, but she didn't, so she asked, "How does that sound?"

"Okay" said Joyce, softly. Her voice was barely audible, even in the quiet space of the garden room, Rachel had to lean forward slightly to make sure she caught Joyce's words correctly. "That sounds alright." Her eyes lifted slightly as she looked at Rachel and immediately fell back down to focus reluctantly on the circle of gold around her finger. Rachel was fervently wishing she could transfer some self-confidence into Joyce's fragile psyche.

Instead, Rachel sat back pressing her weight on the cushions placed on the chair for that very purpose and waited for Joyce to begin.

"I'd like my husband to stop beating me."

As she said this, Joyce looked directly into Rachel's eyes for the first time and as she did so, she rolled the sleeves up of her pale blue blouse and showed Rachel her left arm. It was full of bruises at different stages of development. Some were old and yellow, some were vividly purple, most were finger and thumb sized, grouped together where her husband had squeezed too tightly for too long. She lifted the collar of her blouse away from her frail neck and showed her yet more bruises, all hidden just below the line of her collar. Her husband clearly knew what he was doing when he expertly inflicted pain on his wife.

"When I got married, it was for life." Began Joyce, "no one got divorced in my day. My mother had lived a miserable life with my dad and I was expected to do exactly the same. I was taught as a young girl that your husband was your master. You did exactly as he said and you didn't question his judgement."

Rachel shifted her weight ever so slightly, she hadn't wanted to do anything that might have discouraged Joyce from continuing.

"I did love him, once. We were young when we met and I thought he was my knight in shining armour. He took me away from home so it felt like I was being rescued, it's just that when I got to his palace, he turned out to be a toad." Rachel nodded as Joyce finally found her voice.

"I was bright enough to get into grammar school. My mother told me she had no idea how I'd managed to pass the entrance exam. The nuns who taught me often asked me how I'd managed to get in too. School wasn't a place I felt I belonged to particularly and leaving with a qualification in secretarial studies was all that was expected of me so that's all they got from me. Qualifications were wasted on girls like me, I was expected to get a secretarial job, find a man who was prepared to marry me and give up work to have children. My role was always to serve my husband and put up with my lot.

When I married Brian, on the night of the wedding he told me I didn't need to work again. He said he would look after me and provide for me the way a husband should. I laughed and told him I quite liked my job and didn't mind working until we had children. That's when he first pinned me up against the wall and almost spat in my face as he told me that no wife of his would ever work. No one would think he wasn't able to provide for me or any children we might have. You see, he'd been taught that his role was to be the provider. He had to work to put food on the table and any man who wasn't able to do that, was not a man at all."

"I'm sorry to hear that Joyce. What a terrible way to begin a life together." Rachel's stomach churned. She had once felt the same crushing disappointment in her first marriage. Her mouth went dry as the dark memories flashed across her mind and she took a sip of water. "Are you happy to continue? This sounds like it's the first time you've talked to anyone about this." Rachel prompted Joyce, hoping she would continue.

Joyce didn't need prompting, she'd got started and was going to tell her story now she had been brave enough to begin.

"Like a good wife, I apologised and told him I'd give up my job as soon as we got back from honeymoon. Something died inside me that day, but I loved him dearly and wanted more than anything to look after my man and make him proud of me and our new home.

For the first few years, married life was ok. Brian was attentive and caring. He did provide for me and I cleaned, washed and cooked for him. He'd sit and watch me have a bath, telling me how beautiful I was and how he was the luckiest man in the world to have met me andmarried me. He'd always tell me that no other man could ever have me and I was his forever." There was a pause as Joyce sat up slightly straighter. Her face lightened and for the first time Rachel could see there was a glimmer of a sparkle in her pale blue eyes. Even her voice had altered, it was a little deeper. Rachel found herself imagining the very confident young woman that Joyce must have looked and sounded like when she first met Brian. Being the young bride that everyone envied had been a familiar feeling to Rachel.

"How did that make you feel?" Enquired Rachel, rather tentatively. She'd had her own experience of a man who wanted to watch her in the shower and the bath. It had got to the point where she'd had to go to the gym to find time to be alone. He'd used the excuse of enjoying watching her, but it became part of his control. He'd often told Rachel that now he was her husband, he owned her body. A chill went down Rachel's spine as she pushed the disturbing pictures out of her mind and re-focused her attention on her client.

"This was the most romantic thing I could imagine." Continued Joyce. "I felt so special to be his wife. I enjoyed his attention and ignored the nagging doubts that were beginning to emerge." Joyce stopped again. Sighing heavily. She then took a large breath and pushed her shoulders back and as she did so, she gripped her hands tightly together, holding onto herself for strength.

"It took a good couple of years before Brian gained full control of my life. He'd give me the housekeeping and expect receipts for everything, checking the cupboard contained the things I said I'd bought.

I was never allowed to bathe by myself. I remember him checking the bath when he came home from work one evening to discover it was wet. I'd cleaned the oven and needed to wash away the grease and grime from my skin. He came slowly down the stairs and walked up to me in the kitchen, grabbing a clump of hair at the back of my head, pulling my head right back.

I told him he was hurting me and asked him to stop. He didn't, he pulled harder and the pain shot through my neck, down to my feet. He told me that he must always be in the room when I have a bath because it's his right as a husband to always know what's going on with my body. He told me he owned every part of me and promised to inflict worse pain on me if I ever took it upon myself to have a bath without him being present again."

It had never occurred to Rachel that there might be a pattern to this type of controlling behaviour. She mused upon how many other women were unable to spend time alone in the bathroom bathing without having a man monitoring their every move?

"It sounds like you've had a tough time with Brian. How long have you been with him? How long has this been going on for?"

"For three decades now I have put up with Brian's fists coming at me when I least expect it. I've been at the sharp end of his tongue more often than I care to remember. It's become 'Brian's way' of doing things. I've made every excuse under the sun for him. We had one child, a son. He was clever and left home to go to university as soon as he could to escape his father's put downs and taunts.

"Joyce, I'm going to ask you this question because it helps me understand the dynamic of your relationship with Brian. It isn't a question designed to accuse you of anything. Is that ok?"

"Yes"

"Did you ever defend yourself when Brian was attacking you physically or verbally. I want to emphasise again that there is no judgement in asking you that question." Rachel hoped the question would give Joyce an opportunity to express some degree of strength or self preservation. She knew from her her own experience, fighting back physically wasn't an option and in the end, she had been too exhausted to retaliate with words."The only time I defended myself was to protect our son. Brian was so angry, he broke my arm. As I raised my arm above my head, standing in front of our son to protect him. Brian took the rolling pin and hit my arm so hard you could hear the crack. Just that once he slipped up, I almost got away. I had to go to hospital and the nurse asked me at least three times how I'd broken it. My story of tripping on a rug in the hallway stuck in my throat, but I managed to convince her long enough for her to discharge me once she'd put the plaster on. Brian had put on his loving husband act in front of her, but I know she saw through it."

Joyce had rubbed her arm absent mindedly and she carried on with her personal history.

"I'm not sure it would have made any difference anyway. In those days, it would have been described as a 'domestic' and the police wouldn't have taken me seriously."

Rachel had known that times hadn't changed much in recent years. She'd received threats of violence from her now ex-husband in the first year of their separation. Through her work as a therapist, she understood that it's during the first year of separation that a woman is most at risk of being seriously injured or killed by a former partner. In

Rachel's case, the police officer on duty at the front desk of her local police station had dismissed the texts she'd shown him and informed her that his hands were tied. He'd informed her that her estranged husband would have had to 'commit an offence' for the police to get involved.

Rachel had made it clear that he'd already been violent towards her, once in front of the children. The officer was unimpressed and suggested she make a formal complaint next time it happened. Not for the first time in her life, Rachel had realised at that point she was very much alone in the world.

Joyce was right. Even if she had left when Brian broke her arm, where would she have gone? How would she have supported herself? She'd have had the clothes on her back and no more. She would probably have lost contact with her son too.

"Yes, I think you have a point Joyce, I'm sorry to say." Rachel had no comfort to give. She wasn't sure if times had changed, perhaps women were treated better now. She sincerely hoped so.

"From time to time I would meet with the one friend I had and she would beg me to leave Brian. She could see how miserable I was, despite the permanent brave face I put on. To this day, I have no idea why Margaret remained patient with me. Losing Margaret to breast cancer hit me hard, so hard that it finally started to make me think about myself. I knew I didn't want to die whilst Brian was still my husband. I couldn't face another ten, twenty or thirty years of him. I'd given up hoping he would die. He just seemed to get stronger and stronger. His physical job kept him fit and he was always careful about what he eats. He doesn't smoke and he only drinks at the weekends, so I couldn't see a way out."

Killing your abuser was an option some women chose. Rachel knew that, perhaps better than anyone else.

"I'd stopped loving Brian a long time ago. With each punch, pinch, cruel word and put down my love for him diminished inch by inch until there was nothing left but fear. I could have kept going, but something began to change when I went to Margaret's funeral.

"It was one of the very rare occasions that Brian had let me go to a social function on my own where there would be a crowd of people he didn't know. In particular, he didn't know the men that would be going and he didn't like that. He'd asked for time off work on compassionate grounds, but his boss had turned him down telling that, 'Your wife's best friend dying isn't a good enough reason to give you the morning off Brian.' He didn't like that and I'd knew there'd be consequences for me after the funeral."

Rachel nodded, as she knew full well that anything that went wrong in the abuser's life was always taken out on the abused.

"I didn't mind going on my own and told Brian that I would be fine. He reluctantly let me go. I knew there would be hell to pay when I got home and so I was nervous throughout the funeral. People I hadn't seen for years commented on how upset I looked, assuming it was because of the circumstances. I stayed as strong as I could for Margaret, but I felt she kept looking at me from her coffin, searching for those signs she'd seen so many times before. It was raw fear she saw, exactly like the sheer terror I was feeling now. Like the dark eyes of a frightened animal, my pupils widened at the thought of going home to Brian and enduring the consequences of my flirtation with freedom."

Rachel had finally seen a glimpse of the articulate, intelligent woman that Joyce had described herself as earlier in the session. There was someone inside the shell that had a strong will and strong mind. Rachel hoped that this small kernel of self-belief could be nurtured to grow.

"Whenever Margaret and I met, I would always say goodbye and promise to catch up with her the following week for a coffee at my house. Going to cafes always led to a whole list of questions from Brian. He insisted on seeing receipts for the items I'd drunk or eaten, saying it was his right because he paid for everything. There were no arguments I could think of nowadays that got me anywhere other than pain so I accepted his terms unhappily whilst smiling and reassuring Brian that this was only fair and that he was right.

"I can't believe Margaret kept coming round all those years. It must have been so tiring to keep hearing the same things every week. I would try to divert the conversation away from Brian's behaviour towards me, but Margaret saw straight through me. She must have had the patience of a saint. She never gave up on me and sometimes I think our weekly coffees kept me alive. There were many times I wanted to kill myself. I'd thought of how I would do it too. The idea of leaving my son alone in the world, with no other family than his father, kept me going and the friendship I had with Margaret got me through life one week at a time."

"Joyce, you've been very brave coming to see me today. You've been strong and held things together for your son. You've done what you felt was right for you at the time and no one, but you, knows what you've been through or how you feel. Many people who've been abused blame themselves. This is what the abuser wants you to do. Perhaps the first person you might want to forgive, is yourself." This wasn't so much of a question, than a command that Rachel fervently had wished Joyce would accept. Maybe not now, but soon.

Joyce continued, her voice becoming more animated and louder, something Rachel felt was significant. She knew that keeping your voice low and quiet was a way of hoping your abuser couldn't hear you, wouldn't notice you and would leave you alone. If you were too loud, then he'd bound to be more aware of you.

"I often heard the words coming out of my mouth and wondering who was speaking them. I always sounded so pathetic, so weak and needy. I was strong once, an independent woman with a mind of my own. The person who lives with Brian isn't the real Joyce. It's the shell of Joyce. All that's left is my body because my mind has disappeared and whatever you might think a soul is, has also vanished, a long time ago. I don't know who I am anymore. There are no signs left of that independent Joyce. Margaret had been my only link to my life before Brian and I'm so grateful to her, although feel guilty that I never told her or thanked her. Now it's too late. Maybe Brian's right, maybe I am useless."

The shell of Joyce sagged deeper into the chair. Her body looked like an old empty sack. The edges were badly frayed and the contents had been raided by savage forces, one of which was time. It had not been kind to her, making her look worn out with the effort of living.

"You're not useless Joyce. You've a survivor and you're here, now, telling me your story, which I am grateful for. It also tells me how brave you are Joyce."

"Brian didn't seem to notice that I'd disappeared as a person and become a shadow. He only heard what he wanted to hear and only saw what he wanted to see. He always had very good logical explanations as to why things had to be the way they did. Even though I felt his logic was flawed, I didn't have the energy to fight it. How can someone argue against pure logic with feelings?"

It was though history was playing out in front of Rachel. She understood from personal experience, the hellish frustration of not being able to reason with someone who twisted and turned everything you said. It left you with nowhere to go. Retreating into your own mind was the way Rachel had dealt with it. Pushing the anger down inside you, behind double thickness steel doors of emotional armour plating was the way she had coped. She knew though that the slightest reminder of her predicament; the changing colours of autumn leaves, the smell of the changing season from September to October would trigger traumatic memories in her: namely of feeling utterly helpless and alone in the world.

Her ex-husband had a knack of making her feel that her thoughts were messy and illogical. She, like Joyce had got to the stage where silence was preferable. She no longer allowed herself to acknowledge her emotions, it was too risky. She had been that numb woman existing in a joyless vacuum. Rachel silently thanked herself for leaving when she did and considered the way Joyce had felt duty bound to stick with her man, no matter what.

"Brian kept everything filed away, literally. He had files for my activities, for the house, for his job and for our holidays. Receipts were logged on Excel spreadsheets stored on his PC and hidden behind passwords he didn't share with me. Bank accounts were opened in joint names, I know because I signed papers, but I was never allowed to access them. Brian told me that the money was safe and he took care of it just like he took care of everything else.

"We went on holiday at New Year. Brian had found a deal and booked it as a nice surprise for us both. He said he wanted to see the sunshine in the winter and avoid the annual depressing festival of turkey leftovers, faded decorations and wandering around the sales in dark, dismal weather with hundreds of other people who didn't know what to do with themselves between Christmas and New Year.

"I liked the idea and wondered if a change of scene would help ease my tensions. My headaches were getting worse. The pain in my head was now almost constant.

"The airport was full of happy looking families heading to the sun for the same reasons as Brian and I were. I noticed a family of four: the mum, the dad and the two kids. The mum looked at me. She looked right into my soul and saw my pain. It brought me out in goosebumps and I looked away ashamed. She'd seen Brian in the queue for sandwiches and watched him as he got aggressive with the checkout girl who couldn't find the right change for him. He always had a short fuse. He called it 'not suffering fools gladly' claiming his higher levels of intelligence meant he got frustrated with 'stupid' people. He thought I was stupid and that's why he got angry at me.

"This mother, wife woman, saw Brian and then saw me watching Brian. She recognised the fear in my eyes, she saw my hands twiddling the tassel on my handbag and noticed the red flush of embarrassment rise up from my chest through my neck to my face. She looked back at Brian with disgust and drew herself up higher, standing close by him in the queue. Inside, I was pleading with her not to say anything to him. She didn't know what he was capable of and I knew I would be living through the consequences later if she caused a scene.

"We got on the plane. It was one of those cheap flights where you had to fight to get to sit next to the person you were travelling with. I saw the mother again. She had reserved four seats in a row with bags and was signalling to her husband to bring the two children back down the aisle of the plane to take up the seats.

"Brian challenged her by saying, 'I didn't know you could reserve seats.' His tone was as aggressive as usual and loud.

"She replied 'I'm reserving the seats so we can sit with our daughter and our son.' Her tone was firm and as loud as Brian's.

"She was taller than Brian and quite well turned out, the family obviously weren't poor, but they weren't rich either, otherwise they'd have flown on a nicer airline. He begrudgingly backed down and the mother sat her family down in the row of seats she'd saved. She'd stood up to him and won.

"Why couldn't I be more like her. Why can't I stand up to Brian? What's stopping me from being like her? I spent the whole week going over this in my head. That woman had looked at me and known what I was experiencing. She saw straight through my compliant smiles and saw Brian for exactly what he was. How did she know? Who else knows? I'd been telling myself for years that if I kept it a secret, that it didn't really happen. If no one saw the bruises, then they didn't really exist.

"We celebrated New Year's Eve like everyone else in our resort and went back to our room slightly drunk and relieved it was all over for another year. Brian picked a fight which is what he usually did after we'd been out and had a few drinks. I can't even remember what the problem was. All I remember is having an unfamiliar feeling in the pit of my stomach which told me to fight back. Something stirred in me that I hadn't felt for years. Somewhere inside me was a tiny morsel of strength. I pictured the woman on the plane and used her voice to contradict Brian.

"It was me who spoke, it wasn't the old, long-forgotten Joyce. It was this woman from the plane. I used her courage to stand up to Brian. It felt good, it felt like I was gaining some control back. Maybe it was the alcohol that gave me false courage, I don't know, but what I do know is that something finally snapped.

"The next day we were due to fly home and I had to wear my dark glasses, even inside. For once Brian had lost control of his fists and hit me square in my eye. Our flight was in the evening and by the time we got to the departure lounge, the deep purple bruise was forming like the black patch on an ink-stained sheet all around my eye and cheek.

"I had to take my dark glasses off at passport control and explain that I'd walked into a door in a drunken state after New Year celebrations. The boarder guard had seen too many drunken Brits to care and cleared me through Passport Control. Besides, why would anyone bother about a simple domestic between husband and wife.

"Brian carried on with the tale to anyone who would listen and I breezily wandered through the airport, laughing at Brian's story of my clumsy misfortune. Then I saw her.

"The woman with her husband and two kids were on the same return flight. She looked at me, her eyes scanning my disfigured face. She smiled very gently at me and I could feel her sympathy from across the departure lounge. Then she turned her head sharply towards Brian. I'll always remember the look of contempt that was written across her face, she glared at Brian, looked him up and down and nudged her husband as she whispered something to him. He shook his head and gently held her arm to comfort her. If she'd had any doubts before, she now knew what Brian was and what I was.

"I couldn't stand her pity and couldn't bear to think that a complete stranger knew my story. I stopped pretending to myself that my relationship with Brian was normal. I stopped telling myself that he would calm down one day and stopped believing that if only I didn't do anything to upset him, everything would be ok.

"None of my life had been true since the night of my wedding. I've been lying to everyone I met since that day, to our son, to Margaret and to myself for decades and now I'm exhausted. The exhaustion has finally overcome the fear and I knew that I had to do something to stop it which is why I came to you.

"I saw your photograph in the local paper advertising your counselling services and I recognised you from the airport."

Day Two - Rachel The Daughter

15th December

The kids were on a high because Christmas was on it's way. They were even more excited because a new arrival in the form of a baby brother or sister had been promised for the festive. In the meantime, they had to be content with bikes and the latest electronic gadgets. The eldest, a daughter, was heading towards the teen years and Rachel hoped they would be less traumatic than her own fraught teenage years. An eating disorder in the form of bulimia, feelings of deep depression, thoughts of suicide and a powerful dislike, verging on hatred, of her mother were all markers in Rachel's adolescent years. This, coupled with the violence she had experienced at the hands of her mother, had left Rachel with some serious emotional scars.

Her boy, now eight, currently the youngest and soon to be the middle child, was simpler, more straight forward and Rachel often wondered whether this was because he was male or because he was the second born. He'd suffered none of the angst that accompanies a first born child. By the time Sam came along, Rachel had got the hang of motherhood, as much as anyone ever gets the hang of it. As a consequence, he was laid back, having only ever had one tantrum over a kid's-sized trolley in IKEA. Rachel wondered about the misguided lunatics who created trollies for kids to use in stores and decided they clearly didn't have children of their own. Sam usually went with the flow and so far had given her an easy ride.

Amidst the comings and goings of home life, Rachel was treading the delicate tight rope of her dying mother and trying to balance her work, being pregnant and managing the household. Living two hundred and fifty miles away from her mother wasn't helping the situation. Rachel's husband had been patiently holding the domestic fort for the past three weekends as Rachel made the tortuous road trip to her mother's home.

That home had never been Rachel's. Her mother shared it with her husband, Rachel's step-father. They had moved house every four or five years since Rachel could remember, never settling anywhere for too long. Her mother was one of those people who thought that each new house would bring happiness. Every time she installed a new bathroom or new kitchen, her mother believed she would finally find peace with herself, some kind of inner contentment that put an end to the bitterness and discontentment she experienced every single day of her life.

Rachel was never quite sure what her mother was bitter and disappointed about. All she knew was that she'd taken a lot of her bitterness out on Rachel over the years and would still be doing that if she'd let her. The boundaries between them had been set firmly by Rachel seven years ago when she finally stood up to her mother and told her that some things were none of her business. Her mother hadn't taken it well and still attempted to prize choice pieces of information from her daughter, ready to be stored up and used to criticise her and undermine her at an unspecified later date.

Today was Saturday and Rachel was gearing herself up mentally to face the four hour trip to Manchester. She hoped that Joyce was ok and wondered whether she'd found a safe place to go once she'd decided to leave Brian. Rachel had given her the details of a women's refuge she knew about, understanding that the precise time an abused person leaves the abuser, is the most dangerous. She was genuinely concerned for Joyce's safety and had given her a landline and personal mobile so she could phone or text at any time. In her heart of hearts, Rachel knew she would never hear from Joyce again, there was something that told her she would leave and simply disappear. Rachel didn't blame her. If she had suffered what Joyce had suffered she would move to the other side of the world if she could and attempt to start her life again.

She'd asked Joyce to make another appointment as a follow up because of the deep concerns for her safety, but Joyce has politely declined.

This was the most frustrating part of Rachel's job. She never quite knew whether her clients went onto flourish and succeed, freeing themselves of their trauma, guilt, fear or whatever human emotion was holding them back. All she could do was offer her clients the skills to think differently about their situations and find ways to make things better for themselves. They were all at liberty to ignore her and she often felt that most of them probably did because ultimately, change was too scary or too difficult for them.

Rachel consoled herself that at least she listened, cared and offered tools to her clients so that when they were ready, they could begin to lead fulfilled lives, free of guilt, fear and crippling self-doubt.

Most of the time, freeing themselves meant cutting or reducing ties with close family members, people who had been masquerading as friends or leaving lives that to the outside world seemed "perfect". Rachel had no idea what a "perfect" life looked like, sounded like or felt like, she had no desire to have such an unblemished existence because she knew it was the flaws in her life that had led to her where she was now and that was pretty much ok.

As Rachel drove down the motorway, sitting comfortably in the soft black leather seats of her silver Mercedes, she thought again about the relationship she'd had with her own mother. It had never been easy. They'd never been that mother and daughter combination who went shopping and had lunch together. They were never best friends. In fact, after Rachel's first marriage ended, she'd learned to build those boundaries with her mother, something her therapist had told her at the time would be useful. And she was right.

Rachel's mother liked to control and know things. She wanted to know the details of her daughter's life usually under the pretence of being understanding or helpful, but in reality with the intention of using that knowledge to carp, gripe and above all: judge.

They say that people who are in most need of counselling become counsellors. Rachel often thought about this and knew that her own journey had been very ugly at times. She'd been physically and verbally abused by her mother, except in the seventies and eighties it wasn't called that. In the politically incorrect seventies it had been called "punishment" or "putting you in your place". She could still recall the ringing in her ears after one of her mother's powerful smacks to the side of her head, usually for "insolence" or "disobedience".

Like Joyce, the bruises heal and the ringing stops, but it's the words that stay with you. "Lazy bitch!", "slut", "slag" and "ungrateful cow" were Rachel's mother's favourite phrases which she spat out with poisonous venom: a twisted, ugly expression etched into her face.

Teenage Rachel hated her mother, hated her so much that she lay awake at night wishing she would die. And now she was dying. The first few weekend trips to Manchester had involved house visits, then hospital visits and now it was a visit to the hospice.

There are things that happen to a human body when it begins to die. One of them is the secretion of mucus from your nose. At first Rachel thought her mum had a cold and commented on it to one of the nurses who tentatively agreed. It was a day after this mucus started flowing out of her mother's nose, that she was transferred to the hospice. The nurses had known. They understood that this was the beginning of the end of life.

Rachel loved that phrase, "the end of life" it sounds so much better than dying, but that's the reality. The body decays, withers and shrinks to nothing. The mind of her mother had already faded. The lung cancer had begun to attack her brain, eating away at her thoughts. She'd courageously kept tackling her Suduko puzzles right up until going into hospital. Each day she struggled more and more to complete even the easy ones. It had only been a month before that she could happily work her way through the hard ones. Cancer eats the brain quickly and without remorse. It leaves no cell unturned and corrodes the very core of who we are as human beings, leaving only the spirit to fight on as long as it can.

Rachel comforted herself in the knowledge that the less her mother knew, the better. Her mental state being the saviour of her sanity as she slowly died a horrible, painful death. Rachel felt no sense of "karma" in the nature of her mother's death. She had forgiven her a long time ago as a part of her training and come to the understanding that her mother did the best she could at the time.

Having her own children, made Rachel realise how difficult life must have been for her mother, bringing two children up on her own on a student grant. That student grant had turned into a full time salary as a head of fifth year for a large comprehensive school but that struggle alone had taken it's toll on her mother. Rather than being a positive, optimistic person, the years of financial and emotional solitude had left her bitter and resentful of anyone else's success. It was sad that her mother couldn't or wouldn't see the success she'd made of her own life, maybe she was disappointed in herself. She had no need to be, she'd supported two children, on her own and brought them up to be successful, caring adults who were actively contributing to society.

It's not as though her mother hadn't had therapy either. Rachel remembered her mother returning from a Transactional Analysis weekend holding a poster she'd made as part of her therapy. Her mother had created a collage picture of a blonde, curly haired, blue-eyed girl with pale skin and rosy cheeks, it was the archetypal princess and her mother declared that is how she'd like to be.

Rachel had been utterly confused by this. Her nine-year old brain had been unable to decipher the link between her dark-haired, dark-skinned mother with hazel eyes, large hands and size nine feet. She definitely did not fit the description of your average princess in your average fairy tale.

It was at this point that Rachel knew she was on her own. Her mother had come back from the therapy weekend and declared that, "From now on, it's about me, I'm going to look after number one. It's my time now."

Rachel felt sick. She'd missed her mum over the weekend, having to spend two nights in a damp council flat with one of her mother's friends and her whiny baby. Her older brother had been sent to a friend's house, so at least he was warm and comfortable. Rachel had spent the whole weekend shivering and hungry, the friend had fed her baked beans on toast for two days with very little else to eat and now her mother was telling her she didn't care about her anymore. As an adult, Rachel knew that's not what her mother meant, but as a nine year old child, that's the only thing she could think it meant.

She'd never really forgiven Rachel's father for leaving when she was a baby, leaving her with a four-year-old son and a one-year-old daughter to bring up alone and with no income, other than a meagre grant. Rachel's father seemed rich by comparison and probably more importantly: free. He was free to choose another wife and when that didn't work out, divorce her and choose yet one more wife. Whilst Rachel's mother failed to find love for many years.

In the three years Rachel had been a single parent, she'd gained a tiny insight into the evenings of solitude, weekends and special occasions without her kids and the realisation that financially, she was on her own.

It was during this period that Rachel gained new respect for her mother which might have brought them closer together if it wasn't for her mother's judgements and snide comments about her decision to leave her first husband.

"You must have done something to provoke him." Was a phrase Rachel clearly remembered when she'd phoned her mum in tears after being pushed down the stairs and threatened by her estranged husband. Coupled with, "You must have contributed to his alcoholism, you're not easy to live with you know." Both stung Rachel like a scorpion's tail; excruciatingly painful and long lasting. She'd taught herself to wipe these words from her mind and believe that her mother was speaking from a place of misplaced loyalty to her daughter's estranged husband. She wouldn't allow herself to think that the words were spoken in malice. That was too painful to consider.

Her mother had loved her son-in-law. She'd admired him for being the house husband whilst her, "ruthless and ambitious" daughter had run her own business. She'd sympathised with the man, often asking him how he put up with Rachel's unbridled ambition, knowing nothing of the verbal abuse, the constant criticism, attempts at control and discreetly hidden empty bottles of vodka. No, Rachel's mother knew nothing of that, she only saw and heard what she wanted to see and hear. Don't we all?

Rachel refused to blame her mother for her callous and unthinking comments because no one knew what she had gone through. To the outside world, her first husband was a doting father, a great cook and a modern man who had given up his career to look after the children so his wife could build her business. That's also the story that Rachel chose to repeat to whoever would listen, each time lying to herself, finding it too difficult to think about the truth.

A quick coffee at the best motorway services in England and a bite to eat and Rachel was back in the car, speeding down through the Lake District, over Shap and down to the industrial north. Now, more of a retail north as the old mills had been transformed into executive apartments and shopping galleries full of independent and artisan retailers peddling their wares. The quality of life in the mills had certainly improved, but the north had lost some of its grit.

Rachel went straight to the hospice. A single storey building surrounded by trees, lawns and strategically placed water features and statues to add interest for the residents who in the most part lay in their beds day in, day out, marking out time with carefully prepared meals, and juice from beakers administered by caring nurses until the inevitable happened. The staff were discreet, polite, warm and friendly, making the visits slightly more palletable. Her mother wouldn't be in there for long, no one was. Ten days to two weeks is the average stay and no one walks out of there after being a resident.

The day patients get to leave, the residents who are allocated a room, do not.

Rachel walked into her mother's room, taking a deep breath before she did so and fixing a smile upon her face. She had to be prepared for whatever was going to face her. Her mother lay in a high tech bed, with an array of tubes coming from the cannula on the back of her frail hand. Her mother had once been a tall, powerful woman, five foot nine and around fourteen stone. That full force was behind the hard slaps, no wonder Rachel's ears rang for half an hour after she struck her blows.

Now, her mother couldn't even lift her arm. The nurses regularly repositioned her to avoid bed sores, she had no power over her movements at all: she was utterly helpless.

Rachel's older brother was already there and remarked that his mother's "second favourite child had arrived." It made them all laugh, including their mother who smiled weakly for the first time in a long time.

The family unit of three talked and joked like they had always done in the small terraced house in north Manchester that they'd been brought up in. They'd been a tight unit, facing the harsh, critical world outside; a very traditional world of nuclear families who didn't believe in divorce and thought single mothers were the cause of society's ills. They'd gone to the laundrette once a week together, done the Friday shop at the grotty supermarket at the top of the road together, walking back with plastic bags cutting into their fingers and taken cold, windy holidays in caravans and cottages whenever they could afford it: together.

Rachel's mother had known she was dying for around two months and had already asked her daughter for forgiveness. She admitted she'd been horrible to Rachel as a teenager and she had apologised. Whilst Rachel once upon time had desperately wanted to hear those words, they didn't matter now. Her mother was dying and she knew she had been loved even though that love was sometimes hard to discern.

The sadness Rachel felt was for her mother, the woman who had battled to bring up two children on her own whilst studying for her A'Levels and then her degree lay lifeless in a strange bed. She had sat up to midnight typing her essays on an old typewriter in order to get her degree, trying to juggle the domestic chores of family life and the pressures of bettering herself. Rachel wondered why this had never given her mother a sense of achievement or a belief in her own abilities. Is as though her mother had forgotten her triumphs and only focused on the things she lacked. Three was the constant complaint that she couldn't afford new clothes or expensive holidays. She never seemed to be content. Never ever found peace with herself.

As a couple, Rachel's step father and mother were forever moving house, this was more about her mum telling herself that she'd be happy when she moved, happy when she had a new bathroom or new kitchen or happy when she'd sold the house and moved on. It had never dawned on Rachel's mother that she could be happy now and that happiness came from within. She could move house a million times and live in the most beautifully appointed home and still be miserable because she took herself with her wherever she went.

Instead of refurbishing houses, she would have been better to refurbish her own thinking. In her mother's mind, all rich people were crooks, all business people were out to con you and people who displayed their success in cars or houses were always show offs or no better than they should be. When Rachel's brother had turned up to visit her in his new Mercedes convertible, she had asked him who the hell he thought he was. It hurt him. This was his pride and joy and an outward display of his huge success. He wanted his mum to tell him how proud she was of his achievements, but she couldn't. Her discontentment with herself and dissatisfaction with her lot in life wouldn't let her be joyful for her children.

The irony of this had not escaped Rachel, she had worked with hundreds a similarly minded people and enabled them to see the world differently, allowing more joy in to their lives and finally finding peace with themselves. Her mother had refused all attempts to help. Rachel knew the boundaries were too blurred and professionally, counselling your nearest and dearest was not a good idea, but she had been prepared to don an air of detachment and work with her mother if that's what she had wanted. She did not. Expressly stating that, "she'd tried all that stuff in the seventies and it was all the same". Her mind was firmly closed and so she saw the world as she expected to see it; mean, unfair and against her.

Every minute or so, the clear plastic box at the side of the high tech bed would click. The tubes protruding from it delivering high doses of morphine when it detected levels were low. By now, Rachel thought, her mother would not be feeling a thing. Numb from head to toe, only aware of the people around her bed and the change of light at the window. Most of the time she slept, a heavy, laboured sleep which did not induced opium fuelled dreams. Her breathing irregular and strained, each breath bringing death closer. How many more breaths will she take wondered Rachel. How close to death does she know she is? What's going through her mind?

She detected no fear on her mother's waxen face. Her eyes, when open were heavy with the soporific effects of the morphine, glazed over in a drug-induced daze. Death brings the meaning of life to the fore. It loomed heavily in the room like an uninvited guest, waiting to be asked to sit at the table. There was no resistance from anyone in the room, Rachel and her brother both knew what was coming and wanted to welcome death in, releasing their mother from this no man's land of lying unthinkingly in a strange bed. The woman who vaguely resembled their mother was only just present. Her body was there whilst most of her mind had wandered off, destroyed by the cancer that was at this very moment destroying piece by piece this once strong, brave, single-minded and intelligent woman to a husk.

Rachel didn't believe in God, any god. She didn't believe you went to heaven when you died and she didn't believe in ghosts. What she did know was that people are made of energy and that according to the laws of physics: energy could not be destroyed, it could only change form. Her mother wasn't going anywhere, she was changing form.

A few hours past until Rachel's brother said goodbye to their mother and headed back up the motorway to Scotland. Rachel wanted to stay for a while longer to be alone with her mother and to keep her company. Unless you die peacefully in your sleep, being aware of being alone in death must be a terrible place to be and Rachel wanted to be present, whether she was aware of her in the room or not.

The light faded in the wintery garden outside, no life on the trees and not even a sign of snowdrops yet. The hospice had some tasteful Christmas decorations placed around the building, which contrasted nicely with the almost lifeless garden. The birds scratched about for food, keeping starvation at bay by a matter of hours. The frost had barely melted from the sparse, spindly branches of the tree outside the window. A gift from a family to remember a loved one who had lay in bed staring out of the same window, waiting for death to come. It wasn't bleak, it was natural. It was the natural order of life, we are born to live and ultimately born to die. We cannot live for ever and nor would we want to. Rachel's mother had lived without her younger brother, her mother and her father for many years. She had her children and her husband remaining. She wasn't alone, but it was a reduced family circle she inhabited and to live for ever would be to live way beyond our close family and friends, leaving us lonely. Rachel knew the end was very close for the woman who had given her life, each slow, grasp for oxygen counting down to the very last exhale.

She spoke to her softly by her bedside. Soothing her with hushed tones, gentle words to ease whatever pain or anxiety might be residing in her mind. Rachel told her mother she could now be at peace. She took her bony hand into hers, feeling the paper thin skin and noticing the nails that had needed attention for sometime. The neutral nail varnish her mother had had done four weeks ago, was stubbornly clinging on, a visit to the nail bar was long overdue and would now never happen. She had always longed for elegant nails and somehow, this was fitting for her end.

Her mother opened her eyes and a soft curve appeared at the corner of her mouth as Rachel explained how she had now found peace with herself and with the world. Rachel told her how much she loved her and how she knew she would always be watching her, by her side and guiding her. There was a slight tightening of her grip on Rachel's hand and her eyes closed. Rachel knew this anchor in her universe would never open her eyes again.

Some time passed in that peace and quiet, the slow, regular rhythm of Rachel's breathing, contrasting with the rattling, disturbing breath of her mother who was now ebbing away.

Rachel's step dad entered the room, the pair briefly exchanging the usual pleasantries, hugs and uttered words which failed to express deep sadness in the situation they now found themselves in. With Steve able to take over, Rachel said her goodbyes and left. She knew her mother wouldn't last the night and knew she was no longer aware of what was going on around her. She'd mended the damaged relationship as much as she could. There was nothing left to do now.

As Rachel drove the long drive home, she focused on the family waiting for her. Her stoical husband and her two lively kids, the third one almost ready to make his or her appearance sometime in the New Year. They were what mattered now. Nothing else. She always told them how much she loved them and now she was determined to tell them every single day. To avoid the mis-communication and the misunderstandings of her relationship with her mother was now her sole objective. Thank goodness she had told her mother she'd forgiven her and told her how much she loved her. These were regrets she could never have now and wouldn't want to live with.

At 2am Rachel got the phone call from her step dad. Her mother had finally slipped away. No more pain. Peace at last.

Day Three - Rachel The Friend

16th DecemberSunday was a strangely quiet day. What do you do the day your mother dies? What's normal? Life goes on despite the full stop.

Life did go on. The kids wanted to do what kids do, a little too old for soft play these days, but happy enough to sit in a dark cinema and watch the latest PG movie, released just in time for Christmas and a chance for Rachel to sit quietly for ninety minutes with her own thoughts.

She felt disconnected, the strong anchor to the world that had been her mother was now gone. She felt like she was floating weightlessly through space and time. She had no place. Her role as daughter was now gone. Her father was still alive, but they had never been close, he'd made it clear a long time ago that his allegiances lay with his third wife and the daughter they had together.

No, Rachel felt alone. Even a strained relationship with your mother still constitutes a relationship. Now there was a blank space, a dark void with no safety net, no backstop, no foundation, just an empty void of nothingness.

The kids came out of the cinema, chatting excitedly about the film. Rachel did her best to nod and make approving noises, but she wasn't present.

Her husband had offered to take the kids to Pizza Express for tea so Rachel could put her feet up and maybe get some sleep.

Peace at last.

Twenty minutes into her light snooze, Rachel's phone rang. "Damn!" She thought to herself, "I knew I should have switched it to silent". She'd been so used to having her phone on night and day in case of news about her mum, it crossed her mind that this was another habit she'd need to break.

"Hello?" Rachel tried to sound awake and upbeat.

"Rachel, it's Karen." Karen was barely holding it together at the other end of the phone, her voice faltering even over the few short words she'd managed to squeeze out. "Mike's left me."

Rachel's training kicked in, this wasn't some kind of top trumps of misery, this was a friend listening to a friend who was clearly in shock.

Rachel wasn't in shock, she'd seen this coming since Karen and Mike's early days. He had a history of leading Karen to believe all was rosy in the garden and then dropping a bombshell on her at very short notice. Like the time she'd moved into his executive flat in Manchester, letting out her own tiny flat in a grim part of Stockport and moving her life, lock, stock and barrel to suit him. He'd announced one Sunday evening that his new job was taking him to London and that he'd be moving in less than two weeks.

No discussion, no consultation, nothing. Just a statement. All of Karen's friends had rallied round to pick up the pieces, in particular her best friend Sophie had dropped everything, hired a van and driven like a maniac from Scotland to help Karen move and even drove the van packed full of her stuff back to the parental home. Karen had lived temporarily with her parents until her own flat had become free again. It had been humiliating for her. The shame had been compounded by the fact that Karen and Mike worked for the same company.

It had taken an entire year to recover, to get her life back on track and she was well on her way with a secondment to Los Angeles coupled with a promotion when Mike had got back in touch with Karen out of the blue. Sophie and Rachel had nicknamed him the 'feminazi' because he was vain, looked like a woman and was tall, blond with emotionless cold blue eyes) a phrase, which now had a different meaning and one which Rachel was struggling to surpress.

"Tell me what's happened?" Rachel asked cautiously. She wasn't really up for this, but Karen was a good friend and she didn't want to let her down.

"We were out for dinner last night and just after he paid the bill, he announced he was leaving me. Then he walked out." Rachel could detect disbelief tinged with anger in Karen's voice.

"Did he tell you why?" Karen had given up on any kind of therapeutic approach and was herself staggered by the news. She knew Karen and Mike would split up eventually, but she hadn't thought he was capable of being quite that callous. Rachel hoped Karen hadn't picked up on the edge of sarcasm in her voice.

"No. He just got up and left. I have no idea where he is. I've been sick with worry, I haven't slept, I don't know what to do, I've come back to Scotland to stay with mum and dad with the kids, everyone will think I'm stupid. I am stupid, he must of left me because I am such an idiot. He was always telling me I wasn't as smart as him, we'd just booked a holiday to Mauritius. I thought we were happy. I thought he was happy."

If Rachel didn't put an end to this torrent of emotion, Karen would have continued blaming herself. She interrupted the flow,"You can stop blaming yourself Karen, there are two people in a relationship and if one of them isn't being honest, then how do you expect to know anything. You're not a mind reader." Karen was trying to be as even handed and as calm as possible. Her real instinct was to dig out Mike's number, phone him and tell him exactly what she had always thought of him.

Karen had shared details of her relationship with Mike which had caused very loud alarm bells to go off in Rachel's head. She had often chatted to Sophie about Mike and how controlling he seemed. Karen had been flattered by Mike's insistence on choosing her wedding dress. She'd happily accepted the fact that only *his* friends had been invited to their wedding, with her friends being relegated to a "second" wedding which had consisted of a disco in a draughty hall and fish and chips thrown in as an after-thought. At least Karen had got to wear her dress, or rather the dress Mike had chosen for her, twice.

Nothing was said when they moved down to London and Mike bought the big house in the commuter belt and yet chose to live in his executive flat during the week, leaving Karen isolated in a town where she knew no one.

Their two point four children came along in fairly rapid succession: the perfect combination of a son and then a daughter. Mike still lived in his London flat during the week, whilst Karen struggled with two young children on her own. He was generous with his credit card, allowing Karen to purchase the latest style in home furnishings, wallpaper and kitchen accessories.

Nothing was said when Mike chose to take up golf at the weekends, leaving Karen with the kids for most of the day on Sunday and choosing to return to London on the Sunday night for the rest of the week. Karen never complained. She had Mike's credit card after all.

Rachel and Sophie discussed the situation regularly over glasses of wine and had long ago decided Mike was a selfish bastard who didn't give two hoots about his wife or kids. Karen had confessed to Mike's personal habits, which had included painting his nails, shaving his legs and always sitting down to go to the toilet, even for a pee. The women had decided he was gay or narcissistic, either way, it wasn't going to end happily for Karen.

Karen had also neglected their mutual friend, Sophie badly. She'd not been a good friend to her, despite the help Sophie had given her in her hour of need. When your life is controlled by someone else who tells you your friends aren't as good as his friends, then you tend not to contact them. Rachel had always reassured Sophie and given her insights into how spouses control their other halves, how they isolate their "loved one" from their closest friends so that the controlling partner has ultimate control. It has always been Rachel's opinion that her and Sophie needed to be there when the shit hit the fan. And it was always going to hit the fan.

"Come over for a coffee tomorrow morning Karen." Rachel wasn't planning on doing much, she could barely waddle around the house these days. The baby weighing heavily on her pelvis, as well as squeezing her diaphragm. Breathing was as tricky as walking, so sitting down for an hour so to listen to Karen bemoaning the broken fragments of her cosy stockbroker belt existence was preferable to hoovering.

"I'll get my mum to look after the kids for a bit. I know you'll know what to do Rachel, you always do. See you tomorrow." Karen hung up.

Rachel sat still for quite a while wondering why Karen thought she always knew what to do. She'd made some pretty horrendous mistakes in her own life and didn't feel qualified to soothe Karen's fevered brow.

16th December

With the chaos of the school run over for another day, Rachel got home and made herself a cup of tea. She hadn't been able to drink coffee since she fell pregnant, it was one of the things she couldn't face. She scanned the living room and kitchen to make sure it wasn't too filthy, adjusting a cushion, picking up a stray piece of lego and shoving the Monopoly box under the bureau. She'd visited Karen and Mike's home in the Home Counties once. Mike had been away and she'd taken the kids for the weekend to keep Karen company and give her moral support.

The Farrow and Ball colours blended beautifully with the Aga, solid wood floors and the oak beams. Karen had "made it" if you counted material wealth. She had used her husband's MasterCard with ease, paying for lunch, activities and drinks for Rachel and her kids during their stay. She'd even done a little clothes shopping for herself, spying a pink Joules body warmer in the local boutique, insisting that she needed a new one. Rachel had noticed the blue version of the same body warmer hanging up in the vestibule, but didn't say a word. She did wonder though, what kind of fine line Karen was walking. She had no money of her own, no way of earning it and rarely saw her high flying husband. They led very separate lives. Karen had no idea what Mike was up to during the week. He was rarely in his London flat in the evenings, claiming he had this or that corporate event to attend.

And there Karen was, sitting at home in the big house night after night on her own, caring for the kids, spending Mike's money and being starved of companionship and as it turned out: affection.

Rachel couldn't help feeling that the mistress, for there was bound to be a mistress involved with such a sudden turn of events (whoever he or she was), had a better deal. Karen had gone off sex after the kids. Her confidence was blown as her hips widened and her stomach refused point blank to go flat again. Mike had suggested she get a personal trainer to lose a few pounds. He had, of course, found a suitable one for Karen and organised her fitness regime for her, he'd even started checking the Waitrose receipt for "fattening foods". As Rachel sipped her hot Earl Grey, she wondered how Karen could have been so blind, why hadn't she minded that she was lonely, why hadn't she told Mike where to stick his personal trainer programme and mung beans. Karen used to be a really feisty woman, taking no shit from anyone and here she was, a gibbering wreck with zero confidence.

The door-bell rang and Rachel heaved herself up out of the chair to answer it.

Karen stood on the doorstep, as white as a sheet, visibly shaking. Her eyes were puffy and red and her nose was swollen with constant blowing.

Rachel gave her a great big hug. "Come in love. Sit down. I'll put the kettle on."

"It's Sophie." Karen whispered.

"What's Sophie?" Asked Rachel.

"The other woman. It's Sophie." Karen folded into a pool of heart-breaking sobs. They came from the place inside us that we don't like to acknowledge to often: the raw emotion of a wounded animal. That piteous cry which announces a deep sense of helplessness and vulnerability. Karen heaved the air into her lungs between her anguished cries. Rachel held her. That's all she could do. What do you say to someone who has been betrayed by her husband and her best friend?

"Oh. Shit." Thought Rachel, this is going to take a long time to recover from, if she ever recovers. At least Karen would have the kids. There'd be no doubt about that. Karen wouldn't need to experience the added torment of a man who wanted to take her kids away from her. Life as Karen knew it had fallen apart. That cosy, almost anaesthetised existence was at an end, but her children were safe. You can survive anything if your children are safe. It's when their safety is threatened that action must be taken.

Rachel held Karen just that little bit closer and told her everything would be alright.

Day 4 - The Mother in Law

17th December

Tuesday again. Monday had been a write-off. Rachel was still reeling from the news that Mike had been having an affair with Sophie behind Karen's back. If she felt sick at the depth of betrayal, she couldn't begin to imagine how Karen must feel.

They'd had several cups of tea, cried together, hugged each other and sat in disbelief at the chain of events. It transpired that Mike had left the restaurant at the end of the meal, walked down the road to where Sophie had been waiting in the car to take him back to her flat.

It was going to take years for Karen to get over this. No amount of therapy was going to heal this gaping wound in the short term: time was needed.

The kids were off to school and Rachel's husband was off to work, she had one client in today and then she could relax and put her feet up, which is what she had been supposed to be doing yesterday.

Unusually, it was another older woman. Typically, Rachel's clients were forty-something's having a mid-life crisis attempting to deal with whatever they'd done or not done in their lives. To have two women in the their late sixties come to her in the space of a few days was rare.

This woman wasn't like Joyce. Her clothes were new and reasonably fashionable, the coat was knee length, double-breasted and buttoned up to one side at the front. It looked brand new. She wore pink leather gloves which matched the colour of the buttons on her coat. And her handbag was pale cream leather which a tiny pink detail to co-ordinate subtly with the whole outfit.

Like many women of her age, her hair was cut short. Rachel often wondered why women lost their long hair when they hit fifty. It's as though they decide since their fertile years are over, they may as well adopt a more male hair-cut. Rachel remembered her grandmother's short hair, she'd been to the hairdressers once a week to get it set. There was always a panic when it rained because her grandmother's hair was in danger of losing it tightly coiffured look. It also meant she never washed her hair and was one of the few people who used the little shower caps that hotels feel necessary to leave for their guests. Her grandmother had died fifteen years ago, along with many of the shower cap generation and yet hotels persisted in their provision of disposable shower caps.

Senga sat herself uncomfortably in the large, stylish armchair in Rachel's garden room office. When Rachel had first moved to Scotland, she had never met anyone called Senga and asked the origins of the name: "It's Anges, backwards," was the retort of this particular Senga Rachel had been working with at the time. Since then, Rachel had met a Weymes and an Iona. She rather liked the Celtic names, but hadn't been confident enough to give her first two children such names. Her ex-husband was English, like herself and had been concerned about his family's reaction to such a bold move.

Rachel offered Senga a drink, as she always did, to break the ice. She refused, her shoulders twitching as she did so. Rachel made a mental note of the movement and stored it away in case it happened again.

"Do you mind if I have a cup of tea?" It was a rhetorical question, but Rachel felt it was polite to ask.

"No."

The one syllable response, took Rachel a little by surprise, her clients were more likely to fill silences than create awkward ones. The thought crossed Rachel's mind that she didn't have the emotional strength to deal with a silent, withdrawn client today, the events of the past week or so had taken its toll on her own psyche.

As she made her herbal infusion, Rachel spoke to herself silently, "Keep going Rachel, you've only got a few more clients before you can take time off with the baby."

"Thanks for coming today Senga, what do you need from your session?" Rachel's voice was as even and as neutral as it always was. She'd become very skilled as opening people up gently.

"My son is getting married and I've not been invited to the wedding. He's my oldest son, my youngest did the same to me about ten years ago."

"How does that make you feel?" Asked Rachel. 'Don't judge' thought Rachel, 'don't judge.' Except she desperately wanted to judge, this woman did not come across as remotely friendly or amenable. In the short time of sitting in her presence, Rachel had sensed distance, coldness and a level of emotional detachment she had not experienced in a long time.

"Hell mend them." Senga replied. Rachel could hear the hard, bitterness of her voice.

Rachel decided this was going to be a challenging client who had appeared to teach her something, she wasn't yet sure what that something was, but she was beginning to suspect it had to do with testing her patience.

"Ok. That tells me what you think, it doesn't tell me how you feel." Rachel was firm in her response, but kind in her tone.

"I don't know what you mean?" The flat tone of Senga's voice gave no clue as to how or if she was feeling.

"Well, when you weren't invited to your younger son's wedding all those years ago, can you remember the feelings you had then?" Rachel was attempting to dig deeper to past emotions in the hope that Senga could access those more readily.

Then, the hot lava of anger flowed freely into the calm space of the garden room.

"I don't know why Craig married that woman. She was soiled goods, already had a son to another man and she was looking for a meal ticket. She had her claws into my son before he knew what had hit him. Got pregnant as soon as they were married. I wouldn't be surprised if she'd told him she was pregnant just to get the ring on her finger. Then she gave up work and made sure she was pregnant for the next five years so she didn't have to work. Craig paid for everything, including her son from her previous marriage. He's such a kind man, he couldn't say "no" to her.

"He bought the house, furnished it, bought her a car, paid for her driving lessons. She was told after the third pregnancy not to have another child. The two to Craig had both been Caesarian and she'd been warned her body couldn't take another one, but oh, no she had to get pregnant again, didn't she? The other two were at school and she had to get a part time job to show she was doing something because she certainly wasn't cooking or cleaning for the family. Craig had to make the dinner every night after he came home from work. He'd got a cleaner too because she wasn't doing anything around the house.

She barely drew breath before starting a tirade against the world.

"Now we've got Steven."

"Who is Steven?" Rachel asked, keeping as calm as she could whilst listening to the years of pent up anger being released from this woman's soul.

"He's their last child. He's disabled, starved of oxygen at birth because it was a difficult birth. She'd been told not to have another one and now my Craig is tied to that woman for life, he's too decent to leave her with a disabled child. He knows she can't cope on her own.

"He tried leaving her once and even got as far as finding a place of his own to live. And do you know what that parasite of a wife did?"

"No" Rachel said out loud and inside told herself to, 'be neutral, remember, no judgment.'

"She got herself signed on to the dole and told Craig she'd be sending Steven away to a residential care home if he left them. It broke his heart and hurt his pride so he abandoned his plans to leave and went back. He'll never leave now. He's stuck forever to that woman and do you know the worst of it?" She rattled on as Rachel attempted to respond, but wasn't fast enough, "my oldest son is about to make exactly the same mistake. This one has got two kids. I can't believe how stupid my boys are. Damian's fiancé has two older kids and they've just had one together. A little girl. She's beautiful, but now Damien's trapped too."

"Is Damien the son who is getting married soon?" Rachel wanted to check she was keeping up with Senga's family drama because she suspected, this woman didn't suffer fools gladly and would bite her head off if she got her facts confused.

"Yes. I don't like his fiancé. She's over confident and loud. She thinks she's in control and she interferes with the family business."

"Oh?" Inquired Rachel, "What do you mean exactly by "interferes"." This might not seem like a break through moment, but in Rachel's experience, her clients often used these sweeping generalisations. Digging deeper to understand precisely what they meant by it was usually pretty revealing.

"Well, you know." Senga was temporariliy stumped for words.

"No, sorry, you need to help me understand what you mean specifically, by 'interferes'." Rachel felt at ease now. The pattern was familiar to her now.

"Damien discusses his business matters with his fiancé. She knows all about the finances, the land and how the shares are split between my two sons." Senga's face was contorted with the words. Her expressed revealed the intense dislike of her son talking to his partner and mother of his child about his business affairs.

Rachel was afraid the session was descending into one big bitch about Senga's daughter-in-law and future daughter-in-law and wanted to take things back to focus on her client. She'd noticed that Senga's shoulders would twitch violently every few minutes as she described the actions of her sons in relation to their partners. She clearly didn't approve and this disapproval seemed to have a physical manifestation in the form of her twitch.

A thought occurred to Rachel, "Who or what brought you to see me today Senga?" she hoped this would act like a re-set button and start the session on a new, more positive footing. Rachel was beginning to feel decidedly sorry for the poor women who were sharing their lives with this woman's precious sons.

"My Doctor." was all the reply Rachel was afforded by the truculent Senga.

"Oh, what did your Doctor say to you?" asked Rachel, hoping that she'd get an inkling of what was going on.

"She told me that my headaches aren't a medical matter. They can't find anything wrong with my brain, my spine or my nerves. The Doctor said it was probably psychological and related to stress. I've never heard such a load of nonsense in my life. The woman was almost young enough to be my granddaughter. She told me to come here to see if talking therapy would help. I can tell you right now, it's not going to make a blind bit of difference."

'Well, that told me.' Thought Rachel. "You can leave if you like and there'll be no charge." It was one of Rachel's first principles that clients should actively want to see her. It didn't matter how nervous or reluctant they felt, it was really important they wanted to feel better about themselves or their lives in order for Rachel to open up new ways of thinking for them. Senga wasn't interested in thinking differently, she seemed to be quite happy bitching about her family and making judgements about the people around her, women in particular, it seemed.

"No, I'm here now, so I'll see it through." was the response Rachel wasn't hoping for.

"Ok, so let's start again. And this time, I don't want you to tell me about events, I want you to describe your feelings. I'm curious to know how does not being invited to your eldest son's wedding make you feel. Inside?" Rachel hoped that this obtuse way of asking the question would bypass the 'reasons why' part of Senga's brain and head straight for the 'feelings' part.

"It's hard to say." replied Senga

"Ok, so what's it like? Can you think of times where you've felt similar feelings?" asked Rachel whilst praying that this was the chink in the cast iron, titanium-plated armour she'd been pressing for.

"It feels like it did when my husband left me." Senga looked down towards her hands, for the first time in the session showing a sense of vulnerability.

"How would you describe that feeling Senga?" the question was soft

"Like I've been punched in the stomach and all the stuffing has been knocked out of me. He left me for another woman when my boys had left home. He'd been having an affair for years and everyone else knew about it, except me." Senga still couldn't make eye contact.

"That sounds like a difficult time for you Senga, I'm sorry to hear that. It must have been quite a few years ago, but I can see by your face that it feels quite raw still." Rachel knew she shouldn't be putting feelings into her client's mouths, but this woman needed help to articulate feelings that she appeared to have been storing up for well over a decade.

"It's like it was yesterday. You see, my ex-husband died a few years ago and I never forgave him. I didn't even go to his funeral." The twitch had stopped whilst Senga's body relaxed momentarily, giving herself some degree of comfort.

Senga carried on, "He made me sign papers to do with the business and the house which left me with nothing. I was working anyway, but it meant I had to start again. He bought a big house for him and his mistress to live in and then he got her working in his business with my sons. My sons! He wasn't content to take everything from me, humiliate me and lie to me, he had to have that cow working in the business with him and my boys, day in, day out. Have you any idea how that makes me feel? He never once talked to me about his work, he kept everything a secret from me and now he's sharing everything with some slut who used to work in the pub. That's how they met you know. She was a barmaid. A bloody barmaid. Whore."

The last word was ejected from Senga's mouth with spittle. She quickly wiped it from her bottom lip, looking away as she did so.

Rachel decided the best course of action was to avoid slagging off the mistress and go straight to forgiveness. She suspected the inability to forgive was causing the twitch and the headaches. Holding that much bitterness and jealously in your head for fifteen years really can't have been good for her. For anyone.

"Would you like to forgive your ex-husband? What was his name?"

"Phil. His name was Phil."

"Ok, would you like to forgive Phil?" enquired Rachel.

"Not particularly, but I think I'd better had because not forgiving him feels worse."

"That sounds like a plan. Let's run an exercise which will make it easier to forgive Phil and maybe you can forgive a few other people who you feel have let you down or betrayed you in your life." Rachel figured that if Senga was going to forgive one person, she may as well forgive the rest of the people who seemed to have 'wronged' this woman. She was beginning to feel sorry for her. Living with that much pain can't have been easy.

Rachel worked with Senga and made a little bit of progress. The exercise involved asking someone to imagine themselves sitting in a theatre, alone and inviting people up onto the stage one by one and only letting them off the stage once you have forgiven them. Rachel had desperately tried to do this exercise with her ex-husband in mind. Despite years of imagining him being gently ushered off the stage by an imaginary hand of forgiveness, he had stuck fast like a stubborn blood stain in the middle of the worn boards.

It had been easy to forgive him for the pain he had caused her, but the pain he caused their children was something she could not forgive. She felt fraudulent in her recommendation of this exercise to Senga and gave herself a hard time whilst going through it with her. The stain remained. She was learning to live with it.

"How does that feel now?" inquired Rachel.

"It's ok." said Senga flatly.

"What are your thoughts now on your son's wedding?"

"I suppose he hasn't invited me because I called his fiancé a gold digger. I told them both that I thought she was sponging off him in the same way Craig's wife did. I've not spoken to his fiancé for nearly two years."

"Oh, so do you think Damien is worried that you wouldn't come to his wedding because you don't like his fiancé? What's her name by the way?" so far, Senga had steadfastly refused to name her future daughter-in-law.

"It's Louise and maybe you're right. Maybe he hasn't invited me because I told a few home truths." There was still a harsh attitude, despite the minor progress that had been made.

"Maybe Louise is different to your other daughter-in-law? Does she work?" asked Rachel, hoping she'd hear a more upbeat story.

"Yes, she works. I don't know what she does and I don't care either. Damien still probably pays for everything." The twitch was back in her shoulder. This was going to take more than one session and Rachel doubted very much whether Senga would want to return.

"Perhaps you could hold out an olive branch as it's Christmas? Would that help?"

"I could do. I don't want to spend Christmas with them though. I could apologise to Damien. I'm not saying sorry to her. She might have trapped my son, but I don't need to like her."

"Yes, that's true." Said Rachel. "We can't choose our family can we?" It was a banal thing to say, but Rachel had lost patience with Senga, despite her commitment to remaining professional at all times during sessions. Thank goodness her clients couldn't read her mind.

"No, more's the pity." Came Senga's reply.

"So, can we agree that you will make your peace with Damien, work on forgiving your ex-husband by letting him off the stage?"

"Yes. I'm happy to do that, but I'm not sure what difference it will make to my headaches though. I still think the Doctor is barking up the wrong tree." There was no moving Senga from her position of self-righteousness. The world seemed to be a very black and white place to her. Her judgements appeared to be final, once she'd decided what you were 'like', that was that, there was no going back. Her son's had the misfortune to marry women who Senga had little time for. Rachel did wonder what kind of woman Senga would have had time for and concluded that no one was ever going to be good enough for her boys. She'd had a similar experience with her ex-in laws.

She also wondered what kind of joy and pleasure Senga had in her own life. No friends were mentioned, there didn't seem to be another man on the scene and since she'd retired, there seemed to be very little going on in her life. Rachel was sad. It wasn't good to see people closed down that way. She stopped herself thinking that way as she said goodbye to Senga. It didn't do to get too involved with your clients.

"Will I see you again in a month's time Senga, because there are things that could still benefit from being worked through?"

"No, thank you. I've managed this long, I'll manage a bit longer. There's no point in working things through. When you know you're right, you know you're right. I'll not be going to the wedding and I'll not be spending Christmas with my family, I'll be on my own, I've done it before and I can do it again. It's just another day anyway."

And with that, Senga left the garden office, walked down the path and away through the house towards her small, neat, clean car.

Rachel wished she could have given Senga a hug and told her that whilst love makes you vulnerable, it also makes you strong. She opted for a firm handshake instead and retreated indoors to the comfort of her kitchen, choosing to focus on the myriad of family photos, drawings stuck to the fridge and general clutter of her warm family home.

Should she have told Senga that she might not have many Christmas' left to see her family and share her own story. Her mum didn't have the choice anymore. Sometimes her role as a therapist was incredibly frustrating, she wanted to shake Senga awake and make her realise that time was short and spending time with your loved ones was more important than silly feuds. She wasn't sure whether Senga would have taken any notice anyway, some people just didn't want to be happy. They seemed to get more pleasure out of being miserable and stuck than making the effort to be content. There wasn't a day went by when she wasn't thankful for the life she now had and had come so close to losing, could still lose. Rachel still hadn't heard from her ex-husband for a year. The silence bothered her from time to time. Not knowing if he was dead or alive put Rachel on edge. The idea of him being dead appealed to her, but then ideas always have consequences.

Day Five - The Trophy Wife
18th December

A constant stream of delivery drivers were at Rachel's door throughout most of the day. So far, everything she'd ordered had arrived for Christmas. Now the kids were older, their presents were smaller, but definitely more expensive. She'd managed to find something obscure and hopefully useful for her husband. He was the most difficult person to buy for as he had pretty much everything and anything he didn't have, he didn't want anyway.

He liked to use things until they fell apart and even then wouldn't throw them away. There was a very expensive pair of boots still in their box under the stairs that he had never worn, complaining that his old ones were more comfortable and he didn't want to wear the new ones in just yet. Rachel had threatened to take the boots to the charity shop or sell them on line, but her other half had insistent on the fact that he would wear them at some point in the future.

It was things like this that Rachel had long ago decided to let go of. She had concluded that it was better to be happy than right. It had taken her a while to come to this balanced approach to domestic life because for many years she had felt like the underdog. The ten years of chip, chipping away of her confidence that her previous husband had succeeded in achieving, had taken many years to recover from. For the first few years of her relationship with Ed (he'd been name Edward, but everyone called him Ed), she'd shied away from conflict and been scared to speak her mind.

His unending patience had allowed the real Rachel to emerge, slowly, but surely and with renewed confidence, she now felt like an equal in the relationship. The imminent arrival of their first (and in Rachel's mind: last) child as well as their forthcoming wedding was helping to cement this confidence firmly in place.

It took her a long time to realise that it was ok to argue with Ed. Arguing with her ex had meant violence of one kind or another and she'd had to learn to trust Ed's temperament as much as she'd had to learn to trust herself.

The door-bell rang again, interrupting her thoughts. Rachel heaved herself up from the sofa she'd been dozing on: surrounded by at least five cushions to make the experience bearable. This time, it was Stephanie, a regular clients of Rachel's. She'd first met Stephanie at a networking event in town. Rachel had been through one of her, 'I must develop some more business,' phases and had rather optimistically joined a business networking club. It was at one of the lunches held in the New Town of Edinburgh that Rachel had first met Stephanie.

She had never been invited to call her Steph and so stuck to the more formal Stephanie.

Always smartly presented, cashmere, silk and pure wool were amongst her favourite fabrics. Nothing cheap, everything had a label of one kind or another. Even her yoga gear was top end and contained marino wool and silver. She was always immaculately made-up with beautifully cut hair and manicured nails, Stephanie was the epitome of glamour and elegance. She was tall, slim, quite muscular (she often wore short-sleeved dresses and tops which showed off her toned biceps) and spoke with the softest of Edinburgh accents. She'd been lucky in love and business it seemed, marrying a very wealthy internet entrepreneur and running her own boutique fashion label, which had had some success in London and Paris fashion shows. Apparently, some of her designs had been seen in Vogue last year.

Not that Rachel had seen it herself, this was one of the things Stephanie liked to discuss: her own levels of success or lack of it, as she often saw it. Their sessions didn't so much involve Rachel supporting Stephanie to move on with her life and gain a sense of freedom and purpose, they were much more about listening to Stephanie talk about Stephanie.

This did not necessarily sit well with Rachel's ethical standards. Doing the 'right thing' was something she'd tussled with in the past and successfully or at least partially successfully, put morally ambiguous behaviour behind her. It was hard for Rachel at times not to go to the very dark places in her mind which existed before the middle class idyll she now found herself in.

The problem was that she had met Stephanie via one of those cringeworthy networking events, where the over-enthusiastic host tries desperately to expunge a modicum of enthusiasm from an energy-depleted audience who are there mainly for the food and to speak to anyone they knew, even vaguely. Rachel had initially believed Stephanie's request for business coaching and assistance with growing her clothing empire from just her and one assistant to a real brand. Rachel had set her fees accordingly. Now, the sessions were much more about Stephanie's personal life and her disturbingly wealthy and dysfunctional childhood. The truth was that Rachel had grown accustomed to the substantial BACS payments which regularly appeared in her bank account and didn't have the desire to change the situation anytime soon.

She consoled herself with the fact that Stephanie usually got more than her allocated ninety-minute session. This just about soothed her conscience.

"I know my mother outsourced my upbringing to a series of nannies." This was a favourite topic of Stephanie's and one which she returned to on many occasions. Despite many attempts at encouraging her to forgive her wealthy parents, and in particular her mother (why do mother's get most of the blame?) using various techniques, Stephanie couldn't move on.

"That bitch told those nannies not to cuddle me. They weren't allowed to play with me or show me any affection. One of the nannies told me she had to hide in the bathroom with me to give me a cuddle because the security cameras in my nursery were trained on every second of my waking and sleeping day. Mother would scan the footage to check the nannies were behaving as instructed." Stephanie stared out across the garden, her mind drifting off somewhere, maybe she was thinking about the way she was raising her own children.

"I had ponies, rabbits, dogs and hamsters and wanted to look after them myself. My mother insisted on employing someone to do it for me though and I wasn't allowed to get pet hairs on my designer clothes or get my designer shoes muddy. What's the point in giving your children such things when they're not allowed to play with them?" It was one of Stephanie's rhetorical questions and so Rachel simply nodded.

"I know I'm not the perfect mother, but at least my kids have only had one nanny and she was allowed to show affection to them. They love her more than they love me and spend more time with her when they're back from boarding school than they do with me." There was no emotion in this statement, it was just a matter of fact for Stephanie.

"How does that feel?" Rachel asked

"It's fine. Fergus and I are often away for his business when they're back from school, so Fiona takes up the slack for us. They're happier with her anyway, I only annoy them. It's important that I support Fergus in his work, I need to make sure he's not sleeping with any of those bimbos he meets through business. You know the sort: young, slim, single, clever. They're everywhere now. No, I make sure I'm with him: supporting him."

Rachel suspected that Stephanie's husband, was the same Fergus who was having an affair with a reasonably prominent business woman on his own doorstep. Sasha was young, slim, blonde, but not so clever. It turns out Fergus wasn't in it for the intellectual stimulation. Scotland is a village and if you're high profile, everyone knows your dirty secrets; everyone, except the spouse it seems.

"You must be pleased to have them home for Christmas and have the family together?" Ventured Rachel, rather more tentatively than she had intended.

"Yes, we've got that chef everyone likes coming to cook for us on Christmas Day and then we're all off to that lovely place up north for the rest of the holidays, until New Year when we're back at our chalet in Switzerland."

It was at these moments, that Rachel wished she was charging slightly more than she was.

"So, what would you like from your session today?" She asked

"I think Fergus is having an affair."

"What leads you to believe that?"

"I found a spare mobile phone in his bottom drawer, I was looking for an old receipt and I know he keeps then in his bedside cabinet." Stephanie had the good grace to flush ever so slightly at this white lie she was telling.

"And?"

"And. I switched it on and there were numerous messages from the same number. In fact, there was only one number on the phone. No contacts, no email addresses, nothing."

"Ok. What did the messages say?"

"They were filthy. Whoever this person is they have a very dirty mind and I found it quite shocking that Fergus would entertain such nonsense. The grammar was appalling too." Stephanie seemed most upset by the poor grammar than the content of the messages. She still wasn't showing any emotion. There were no tears, no tantrums. She was still looking directly at Rachel, talking in the way she always talked in her quick, clipped tones.

"What will you do?"

"Nothing."

"Nothing?" Rachel couldn't hide her surprise.

"No, nothing. Fergus and I haven't had a physical relationship for years now and I guessed he was finding solace elsewhere. I had assumed he was seeing prostitutes and paying for escorts when I wasn't around. I could never stand the man touching me. He sweats too much and quite frankly the whole idea of having sex with him disgusts me. We managed two children and that, as far as I am concerned was enough to satisfy the family and his ego."

Rachel believed Stephanie and could see that she didn't miss human contact. After all, a child who is left alone on their play mat to play alone whilst another human being sits and watches and is forbidden to cuddle them or show them any affection, is bound to shut that part of their soul down completely.

"No, whoever this person is, he can have Fergus. I'm the one married to him, I'm the one with the contract which states I get half of everything he owns if we divorce or even the whole lot if he dies. I get the lifestyle, the clothes, the jewellery, the holiday homes and the house here in town. What does his bit on the side get?" Another rhetorical question. "She gets taken out to dinner, bought the odd expensive bag or item of clothing and maybe jewellery and nothing if they split up or he dies."

"That's quite a cold way of looking at it Stephanie. And, you said "he" and then "she"? What about your emotional needs?"

Stephanie chose to answer the last question, expertly deflecting attention away from her Freudian slip.

"I don't have any. I closed those down years ago. When you're brought up the way I was, you are expected from a very early age to 'marry well' and keep your mouth shut. Stephanie was inviting Rachel to question this last comment. That's how it seemed to her at least.

"What do you mean by marry well?" She enquired. Rachel's version of marrying well was getting married full stop. She'd been so surprised when her first husband had proposed on her twenty fifth birthday because she had assumed that no one would want to marry her. It had never crossed her mind that a man would want her enough to marry her. Throughout her twenties and most of her thirties, Rachel had believed that she wasn't worth marrying. After the break down of her marriage to her first husband, the years of coercive control had left her feeling that marrying a decent man wasn't something she was destined to do. That was for other 'nicer' women. Not her.

Not for the first time, had Rachel understood that how you were brought up as a girl and what your mother told you about your worth, had a direct impact on the relationships you sought out and settled for. Her own father wasn't around much. It was the 1970's and he saw his kids once a month. She'd never spent a Christmas with her father and had been denied the opportunity to be a bridesmaid at his wedding when she was six. This had devastated her at the time. Why would a loving father not want his two kids at his third wedding? It had taken Rachel decades to work out that it was his third wife who didn't want his children there. But then why should she take the blame, her father should have made a stand. Should have insisted that his children were such an important part of his life that they must be there. The truth was as hurtful as it was stark: his children weren't important enough. Rachel had felt this keenly throughout her relationships with a variety of men. She had sought out men who perpetuated this feeling of lack of worth and paid the price. Luckily, escaping at the last possible moment. Getting away with it. Just.

Stephanie, however, had been groomed to marry a wealthy man. She had been taught from a young age not to be too clever or too opinionated because no decent man would want her that way. After the numerous nannies, Stephanie had been sent to boarding school and then finishing school. Rachel was aware that she had similar plans for her youngest daughter, refusing point blank, to recognise that she was repeating the cycle of cold, aloof, dysfunctional relationships. Rachel had often considered that if a social worker had seen the lack of affection afforded to such children of wealthy parents, then they would be taken into foster care immediately. Poor people simply weren't allowed to get away with neglecting their children's emotional needs in that way. She could imagine a Stephanie in a very different world, living in a council flat in Glasgow, with an income derived from benefits and men who paid her for 'favours', leaving her baby without cuddles and to play on its own on the play mat for hours on end without interacting with it. But because Stephanie had placed the care of her children with a professional nanny, albeit an emotionally distant one and lived in a mansion and spent time at dinner parties, drinking the best champagne, no one noticed or cared.

Rachel couldn't tell the difference morally, between the two scenarios, except one had money and one didn't. Stephanie had long ago stopped the favours for her husband, but that had not been the case in the beginning. Is sex in a marriage ok, even though you don't love or fancy the person you're with and is sex when you're being paid and not in love and don't fancy the person, not ok?

Rachel had never got to grips with these thoughts and feelings. She'd listened to more episodes of Radio 4's 'Woman's Hour' than she cared to recall and she'd heard the views of sex workers who claimed to feel comfortable with selling their bodies for sex. The very same sex workers had pointed out that women who marry for money are just doing the same as they are, except with one man.

Whilst Stephanie bemoaned the state of her life, Rachel came to the conclusion that there wasn't much difference, but at least Stephanie had a contractual agreement which gave her some level of security. 'Yes,' decided Rachel, Stephanie had the better deal.

"You could leave him." Suggested Rachel.

"Don't be ridiculous. I might be miserable with him, but what would I do? He is my life. I've sacrificed everything for him. Given him children, an heir, provided sophisticated dinner parties for his business associates, travelled the world with him so he doesn't get lonely and kept his dirty little secrets for him. His wife is the only job I've ever had. It's the only role I know. It's the only role I've been brought up to do." The last few words trailed off into thin air as Stephanie's demeanour finally softened.

This was the first time Rachel had seen a chink in the seemingly inpenertrable armour of Stephanie's botoxed face.

There was nothing Rachel could do for her client. Change wasn't something she was prepared to consider, there was too much to loose for her. Sometimes it took circumstances to take a significant turn for the worse for her clients to change. She considered her own decision to leave her first husband. It had taken three years from the time she realised she had to leave. Three years of keeping quiet, of making sure she didn't step out of line, give him cause to suspect or realise what she was planning.

Christ, Rachel had even given birth to their second child during that time. She understood the need to keep the status quo, not rock the boat when so much was at stake. Rachel was building a business, she needed money behind her in order to leave. They'd had a house to finish and Rachel had bided her time, just like Stephanie was doing. She was in no position to judge anyone. She'd had sex every week with her ex-husband, it was part of keeping him mollified: a quick ten minute shag every seven days gave Rachel a hollow orgasm and not much else. She'd learnt to switch off. She'd mastered the art of fakery and in exchange she had a house husband and someone who cooked her dinner every night.

Just like Stephanie, everyone else thought she had the perfect life. They saw the career woman with the ideal man: he was good with the kids, a great cook and seemed to be charming. What they didn't see were the empty bottles of vodka hidden behind cupboards, stashed under the furniture and the debt that was spiralling out of control. No matter how much money Rachel had earned, it seemed to disappear into thin air. It was only later she'd discovered her ex had been spending it on booze as quickly as she had earned it.

The nights were the worst. He'd get so drunk that he became unconscious. He often wet the bed and one night had pissed all over the bedroom floor whilst Rachel's dad and step mum were sleeping in the guest room across the hallway.

Rachel definitely knew what it was like to put on a brave face for the rest of the world. Lying to yourself as much as you lie to everyone else. No, she had no reason to criticise Stephanie. She had every reason to applaud her and support her.

"What's his dirty secret?" This was a genuine question as Stephanie had never offered this information before. Perhaps they were making progress after all.

"He loves rent boys."

"Oh." The rumours of the affair with Sophie the blonde business woman Rachel had heard about must be false. Perhaps they were put about by Stephanie's husband who wanted to seem normal in the business world full of powerful men with powerful jobs and big egos to satisfy, usually with attractive successful women.

"Can we work on this next week Stephanie? We've run out of time. I really think we've made some progress here and would like to continue, if that's ok with you?"

"Yes, I've never told anyone that before. I feel better already. It's ok isn't it? I'm not doing the wrong thing am I? I mean, staying with him? I don't want you to think I'm just in it for the money, there's more to it than that. You can see that, can't you?" Her voice was almost pleading.

Rachel assured Stephanie by telling her own story, with almost all of the details, leaving Stephanie in no doubt, that she wasn't alone in her marriage of inconvenience. There were ways to solve such problems, but Rachel wasn't certain enough that Stephanie wanted to hear those.

Left alone once again with her outrageously large belly and her thoughts, Rachel settled back down onto her pile of cushions and drifted off into a deep sleep, ready to wake in time to do the school run.

Day 6 - The Nightmare

19th December

One of the rules of being a therapist is to have a supervisor, someone you can talk to about your practice and your clients. They're similar to an escape valve: when the heat builds up, therapists seek out the support of their supervisor to adjust their settings so they return to normal and are able to continue their work.

Rachel's supervisor was an old man. He was very short compared to her and his skin displayed patterns similar to the nooks and crannies of bark on a wizened tree. His knowledge of therapy was vast and it always amazed Rachel that whatever she brought to her supervisory sessions, Bill was able to dig deep down into his pool of experience and pull out the gem she needed right there and then.

She was supposed to meet him every six months and throughout most of her practice, this is exactly the rhythm she had followed, finding it to be just the right amount of time for pressures to build up and be satisfactorily released.

This session was earlier than scheduled because Rachel was about to take a break for her maternity leave. That was what she had told Bill. In reality, Rachel was feeling the pressures gathering around her like thunder clouds and had to talk to someone to save her sanity.

There was a time in Rachel's life when she regularly woke in the middle of the night shaking uncontrollably. Her breathing would be quick, erratic and shallow. On occasions she would be convinced that she couldn't get oxygen into her lungs. It would be the same nightmare over and over again. On these bleak nights she felt as though she was being cornered by a malevolent force. A being which hung in the air above her, around her. Forcing her back into a black hole devoid of any light. Threatening her very existence. It didn't have a face or a name. It's presence was sufficient to bring on a full blown panic attack. She could almost smell and taste the bitterness of the bile that clung to her when the dead weight was creeping up on her. It felt like a lifetime of disappointment, of jealousy and dis-ease.

As she was sitting across from Bill in his attractively disorganised home office and describing these feelings to him, she could feel the panic rising in her chest. It was all too easy to re-create these intense feelings and Bill could clearly see what was happening.

"Rachel, it's okay, we're safe in here. I've not seen you like this before, do you want to tell me what's going on?" Bill's voice was quiet, but firm. He was one of the few men in her life who she could really trust. If she was brutally honest with herself, she still didn't fully trust Eddie, her new husband despite the fact he hadn't done or said anything that would erode trust. In Rachel's life, men had consistently let her down, starting with her father. She knew in her heart she could trust Eddie, she just hadn't managed to convince her head yet.

Rachel knew why this dark mass of black tar was forcing itself down upon her. She understood precisely what it represented, who it signified and what it meant. She had spent ten years of her life being scared. Afraid to say the wrong thing, to place a cup or a glass on the table in the wrong place or in the wrong way. Cook the wrong meal, clean up in the wrong way, lay the towels on the radiators horizontally instead of vertically. It didn't matter what she did or how she did, it would always be wrong.

"The nightmares have started again Bill."

Rachel told Bill that she couldn't fathom the reason for it, but then went onto to say, "I suspect pregnancy hormones might be involved. The last time I was pregnant was with Sam and it wasn't a happy time in my life. I think my subconscious is trying to protect me, warn me, show me signs to watch out for to keep me safe." It seemed to Rachel to be a perfectly plausible explanation for her current frame of mind. The real truth lay hidden beneath layers and layers of self-deceit, none of which she was prepared to peel away for herself, let alone Bill or Eddie or anyone else for that matter. Some things had to remain deeply buried secrets.

"You know about my past Bill, don't you?" Rachel was able to detach herself from her distant past enough to be able to talk about it with anyone, even complete strangers.

"Yes. I'm aware of some of what went on Rachel, but I'm interested to know what specifically is on your mind at this point in time. It is my job to make sure your mental health is in good order and that you're not posing a risk to your clients in any way." Bill's calm, soothing voice allowed Rachel to relax in to her story, a story she'd told so many times before and was now beginning to feel like a script rather than a description of real events.

"He only hit me in the first and last year of our relationship. It wasn't the physical abuse that hurt though Bill, it was the emotional torment over the years that really got to me. He knew precisely how to undermine me with words. Towards the end there had been shoves, slaps and fists in my face, the threat of violence was ever present in his manner. There were holes in the walls where he'd thrown furniture designed to just miss her and dents in the wooden floor where objects had been slammed into the ground. I sometimes wish he had hit me because it would have been over and done with quickly. Instead I had the constant feeling that I wasn't safe and when the children came along I knew protecting them was now my first priority.

"You don't have kids do you Bill?"

"No, just nephews and dogs."

"When you are a mother for the first time and you bring your baby home, you suddenly realise that you would do anything for this new human being who has appeared, quickly becoming the centre of your universe. You know you would gladly sacrifice your own life for them and you know you would kill to protect them. The urge to protect my helpless, beautiful girl was overwhelming for me. It rapidly became apparent that it was her father I needed to protect her from.

"Spending your time carefully manoeuvring around another person's emotional state is exhausting. He'd go for months without drinking and I would begin to relax. His moods would then to return to normal and I would imagine that I had my loving husband back and dare to believe we could live happily ever after. Then he would decide to have a bottle of cider one night and I knew the pattern would begin again. The cider led to wine, which led to vodka and to the foul moods. Tip toeing around the house became second nature to me.

"He had chipped away at my well-being, Bill, each barbed comment diminishing who I was piece by piece. It was in the sixth month of my second pregnancy that I knew I had to leave. I had no idea how I would leave, but I knew I had to go in order to protect my toddler and my unborn child." Rachel stared into the distance, not sure whether Bill wanted her to go on. She thought she had told him all of this before, it had been part of the process in Bill's assessment of Rachel's suitability to be a therapist. She didn't like going over old ground, but it was preferable to coming clean about what was really on her mind so she continued.

"He was sitting watching television all afternoon one Saturday, drinking orange juice, or what he claimed to be orange juice. I had long ago worked out that the glass contained ninety percent vodka and only ten percent orange juice. I made him promise to stop drinking, but I didn't really believe him. He'd promised before and always broken his word. He'd left me to entertain Rosie, our young daughter whilst I attempted to put a small bedside table together. I knew better than to challenge him. I understood that asking for help from him was only going to lead to more verbal abuse." Rachel paused for breath.

"What kind of things did he used to say to you?" Bill gently enquired.

"When I say it out loud Bill, it doesn't seem too bad. This is what was so hard to explain to my mother and my friends. There was never one thing that he did, it was a whole series of tiny comments, minute jibes and hints of violence that kept me on edge. It makes you think you're the one who is going mad. It makes you believe you're wrong almost all of the time and it means you don't trust yourself to have a proper thought of your own."

"It might help you Rachel if you can give me an example. It sounds as though something is still sticking in your unconscious which needs to be released." With his kind encouragement, Rachel went on.

"The last argument we had, involved him berating me throughout the house. Luckily, our child was asleep in bed upstairs and Sam hadn't yet been born. I had attempted to agree to disagree with him. I honestly thought that if I just agreed with whatever he was saying, he would give me peace. I had walked away, quietly hoping he would leave me alone. I even switched the TV on and shut the living room door in the vain hope that he wouldn't follow me. He did though. He followed me wherever I went in the house, starting the argument over and over again. Locking myself in the bathroom didn't help either, he just stood outside of the door shouting at me, telling me I had no right to an opinion of my own because I was his wife. I had no idea what we had argued about in the first place. It wasn't about that anymore though. He had to win. He had to have the last word.

When he told me that I wasn't allowed to have a different opinion to his I was stunned. He actually told me that I had to think the same way as him and his insistence on following me angrily around the house was to make me acquiesce. I am a strong, intelligent woman Bill, and I was determined to keep my mind in tact along with my opinions. He had taken almost everything else from me and I was clinging onto my sanity by a single thread."

"You are sane now Rachel. You got out. You saved yourself and your children. You did the right thing." Reassured Bill.

"Maybe. Don't we become therapists in order to heal ourselves first?"

"Perhaps. You seem to be in a good place these days and until you mentioned the return of your nightmare, I would suggest you had succeeded in healing yourself Rachel."

Rachel appreciated Bill's positivity. She knew more of the truth than he did though and so readily accepted his version of events.

"I interrupted Rachel. Sorry. How did this argument resolve itself? Were you locked in the bathroom for long?"

"No. He promised to leave me alone if I came out of the bathroom. He didn't stop though. He started the argument again and in desperation, I grabbed the car keys and ran from the house, jumping as quickly as a pregnant woman can, into our family saloon and attempted to drive off. He'd followed me onto the drive. He actually stood in front of the car, blocking my way. He was terrifying. His eyes were full of hate. I didn't want to leave Rosie in bed with that man roaming around the house alone, but I had to escape because I had no idea what his next move was going to be. That was the first time it had crossed my mind. I could put my foot down and that would be an end to this living hell. I quickly ran through the ramifications of this thought and there was no way that I could make that look like an accident. The neighbours would have heard something and I would not be able to explain why I accelerated when my husband was standing in front of the car.

"The truth of it was Bill, that I thought about killing him. It wasn't a rash thought, it entered my head in a cool, calculated way. My thoughts actually slowed down as I mapped out my chances of success. It frightened me Bill. I'm not a killer. I think that's what my nightmare is about." Rachel looked down at her hands in shame. She'd never admitted this to anyone before. It had always been part of her story that she'd missed out, glossed over and moved on from. Most people were too busy feeling sympathy for her to dig deeper into this picture of a pregnant woman desperate to escape the emotional torment of her husband.

"You didn't kill him Rachel. You know that having thoughts and acting upon them are two very different things. We all have dark thoughts. Being able to recognise them and put them to one side is what separates us from the murderers."

"You're right Bill." Nodded Rachel.

"So, what did happen?"

"I edged the car forward and eventually I was able to break free and escape to my brother's house, around two miles away. He calmed me down and told me that no one should have to go through what I was going through. At the time, this hadn't made sense to me. I thought that every relationship had moments like this.

"I went home feeling stupid. I thought I'd probably blown things up out of proportion and overreacted. My eyes swollen with tears. I remember having this feeling in the pit of my stomach like a tight knot. It had been growing for some time and caused me physical pain every time I approached my house. It wasn't home for me, Bill. It wasn't safe or loving. It was a roof over my head and the heads of my daughter and my unborn child."

"What happened when you got home?"

"He'd shut himself away with a bottle of vodka and so I crept quickly and quietly back into the house, scuttled upstairs like a guilty teenager and hoped that his attention was now focused on something else.

I knew there would be no point in discussing the argument. He never remembered anything. He would remember things in a way that suited him and forget everything else. His memory and cognitive abilities were fading with each drink he took and yet he had no awareness of it. He took absolutely no responsibility for his actions and always had to be right.

"I felt I was going mad Bill. I was often left questioning my own ability to remember things correctly. It was getting harder and harder to tell the difference between his reality and my own. It was one of these moments, whilst I was varnishing the bedside table that I knew I had to leave.

"He shouted at me from the living room 'You're not doing it right. You never do these things right. I don't know why you're bothering to do it at all. We don't need a bedside table. You've wasted more money on things we don't need. Your stupidity is never ending Rach, if only people knew what I had to put up with. Stupid woman." His words were sharp, each phrase bit into my flesh like little needles. I was so exhausted and wanted to cry, but couldn't quite muster the energy to produce the tears.

"I finished varnishing the table and looked at my beautiful daughter and knew I would have to leave."

"You were in a difficult position Rachel, it must have been horrible for you." Bill's kindness was almost too much for Rachel and she struggled to keep her emotions in check.

"I have a fantastic life now Bill. All of that is well and truly in the past. Eddie is a fantastic man, he's reliable, kind, loving and a great step dad to the kids. He's excited about the baby too. We have our ups and downs like every couple does, but at least I can talk to him and he listens. I count myself as one of the lucky ones. I escaped. So many women don't get away or by the time they do free themselves and their children, their too damaged to make a decent life for themselves. I remember my best friend telling me once that the mental hospitals were full of women who were wives and partners to drug and alcohol addicts. I can well believe that." Rachel looked around Bill's untidy study, noticing the titles of the books on the shelves. His tastes were varied and Rachel could imagine herself spending an entire day browsing through the most interesting titles.

Whilst Bill talked about the healing journey, Rachel's thoughts wandered into her therapeutic training. It had taken her on a long and often painful journey to uncover the reasons for her marrying an alcoholic. She understood that not having a father at home hadn't helped and the terrible relationship with her mother during her teenage years were all contributing factors. She'd been very young. She had no idea what an alcoholic was. She, like most people thought they were the tramps you saw on park benches drinking cheap cider from a bottle. She never thought they could hold down a job, have a mortgage and live what seemed to everyone else like a normal life.

She felt her baby kick inside her. It reassured her that all was well and this baby would have a very different start to her first two. Her second child, a boy had almost died at six weeks old. Rachel had been exhausted with breast feeding during the night and had gone to bed at eight, leaving her fragile baby boy with his dad. She'd made him promise to stay sober and stay awake and left the pair of them sitting on the sofa watching TV. She'd fallen into a deep sleep and was woken by the soreness of her engorged breasts. Sam's feed was long overdue. Within a split second, she knew instinctively something was wrong and ran downstairs to find her then husband collapsed in an inebriated heap in the corner of the sofa with no sign of their new born child anywhere.

"Are you ok?" Bill's question suddenly interrupted her thoughts.

"Yeah. I'm ok. I'm always ok. You don't get out of a situation like the one I was in without being affected Bill. I know he can't hurt me now. I know it's over." She didn't want to talk anymore to Bill about the old days, it was enough to recall them mentally. Saying them out loud seemed self-indulgent and unnecessary to Rachel now. She knew there were plenty of people in the world who had suffered much more than she had.

Her supervision was over and she gave Bill a hug. She put the next date for her next supervision session in her diary and as she did so wondered what circumstances she would be living in by then. Her third child would be around six months old and she hoped they would all be living a safe, secure life together.

On the way home in the car, Rachel had time to finish her thoughts about that terrible night. She physically shivered as she remembered the blind panic, noticing that knot re-appearing in her stomach as the memory played out.

She'd shifted the dead weight of her comatosed husband, finding her darling boy crumpled beneath him, almost suffocated beneath his weight. She'd grabbed Sam, checked him over and found him to be completely unharmed. She held him very tightly and promised she'd keep him safe from now on. After placing him carefully in his Moses basket upstairs, she vividly recalls heading purposefully back downstairs and marching into the living room where her useless husband lay in his drunken coma. Her basic maternal instincts had fired up deep in her belly and she clearly remembered seeing red before she punched him in the face as hard as she possibly could. He hadn't flinched. Rachel knew in that split second she wanted him to be dead and she had gone to bed hoping that he would choke on his own vomit in the night.

She comforted herself with a new set of thoughts as she glanced down at her ripe belly, wiping the old memories from her mind and knew this baby would be cherished by his or her father. It would be safe to leave the baby with Eddie. Rosie and Ben have a decent step father who would never let them down. She knew she had finally found her home.

Day Seven - The Funeral

20th December

The family needed to be packed into the car, ready for the journey to Manchester. The funeral had been arranged for mid-afternoon so that Rachel and her brother could drive down in the morning. The roads were fairly clear, it was December and the mass movement of people hadn't yet started for the Christmas rush. The weather remained kind too, giving Rachel plenty of time to stare out of the window as Eddie drove.

The kids were quiet; old enough to understand the significance of the day and pick up on the flat energy of their mother. Rachel was physically exhausted and after her disturbed night's sleep, emotionally exhausted too.

She simply had to get through the day and could be back home within twenty four hours, surrounded by her familiar comforts.

There would be people at her mother's funeral who she'd not seen for decades, friends of her mothers who had played various roles in her colourful life. Her days as a part-time bar-maid whilst studying to be a teacher and her days as a left-wing, Guardian-reading activist. Rachel's step-dad had been brilliant, organising things and putting his wife's last wishes into action.

It was to be a wicker funeral casket, with simple humanist service and a few words from Rachel and her brother. Drinks back at the pub in the village where their mother and step-dad had lived for the past twenty years and the only place her mother ever considered home.

The day was drab as only December days can be. No leaves, no greenery, no sun and very little light. Manchester is a damp place at the best of times and the crematorium felt like the coldest, dreariest place on the planet at that precise moment.

It was full. Her mother had known a lot of people. Dying at the age of sixty seven, means there are still plenty of them alive to see you off. Rachel's brother was a fantastic speaker and gave their mother a fitting tribute. Rachel read a poem she'd written, barely able to force the words from her mouth through her stomach-wrenching grief. She was sure this couldn't be good for the baby and so did her best to stay calm. There's no easy way to get through your mother's funeral. People are kind and genuinely pleased to see you. They want to say the right things and reassure you that everything will be ok. You know it will be ok, but right at that point in time, you feel like shit.

Rachel's brother, Steve was older than her by three years. He was an anxious worrier and had desperately wanted their dad to be at the funeral. Steve had phoned their father and asked him to be there. The conversation hadn't gone well and had ended with Steve vowing never to speak to their father again.

Their mother and father hadn't been together for thirty six years and there was no love lost between them. Rachel was the peace-maker and spoke to her dad who made it clear that he disliked their mother and wasn't prepared to attend the funeral of a woman he'd removed from his life, whether she was the mother of his children or not. Rachel knew this wasn't the real reason for him refusing to attend and her brother Steve knew it too. The real reason was because their father's wife (their step-mother) didn't allow him to see his adult children on his own.

Steve and Rachel had enjoyed a couple of lovely evenings with their father in Edinburgh around ten years previously when his business had taken him to Scotland. Neither of them had spent time with their father since playing frisbee in the park when they were little. Rachel had fond memories of her dad picking her up and swinging her round and round by her arms, causing her to scream and laugh with delight. Their step mother had never taken to her step children. She'd got worse since their half sister was born and made sure there was as little contact as possible between them all.

Dad's business trips to Scotland continued, but he was always in the wrong part of Scotland or just over the border in Northumberland so the dinners with his children stopped. Rachel had long ago given up phoning her dad. He always "had to go" because his wife would be calling his name in the background. Rachel had tried calling at different times of the day and evening, but it made no difference, her stepmother always made sure there was something her husband had to attend to when he was on the phone to his daughter.

The visits to his house had diminished too. Rachel had made the effort to see her father one Sunday afternoon after going to a cousins wedding, taking the two grandchildren with her. She'd been made to sit on the lowest chair in the living room, been told that they were going out soon as they had an 'arrangement' and whilst she was offered a cup of tea, neither her step-mother, her father or her now adult half sister were having one, making it crystal clear she wasn't welcome. Her father hadn't even bothered to hug his grandchildren.

She'd left feeling sad. It was the last time she took her kids to see their Grandpa and chose only to visit him on neutral territory once a year at a favourite restaurant of theirs in Manchester. She'd sit and listen to the barbed comments of her step-mother, the strange noises she made under her breath, but loud enough for people to hear, her tuts, her rolling eyes and the constant tapping and nudging that went on under the table with her daughter, signifying various levels of disapproval for whatever conversation Rachel was attempting to have with her father. With a wry smile on her face, Rachel remembered the time her step-mother placed a paper napkin on her head in a vain attempt to draw attention back to her and away from the slither of relationship Rachel was attempting to salvage with her father.

It was Rachel's relationship or lack of it with her father that she often took to her supervision sessions. She'd had to work very hard at forgiving him for his weaknesses. For not standing up to this woman who told him he couldn't have his own children at his wedding. For allowing her to step between a man and his children in so many obvious ways. Not just the foot-tapping and watch-checking she did at those annual lunches, but for the decision to stop sending Christmas gifts, for the electronic birthday cards she'd received via her step-mother's email address and for the fact that this woman attempted to goad Rachel into a fight every time they met. The enmity between them was palpable and Rachel had often spent time with her supervisor attempting to work out how her father was able to ignore all of this. How he was unable to stand up to his wife and lose the joy of the relationship he could have had with his children and grandchildren into his old age.

After living with an alcoholic, Rachel understood their need to control everyone around them and her step-mother was no exception. She had gained full control over her husband and their daughter, but had failed with Rachel and her brother. It was no coincidence that Rachel's ex-husband and her step-mother had got on very well indeed. Rachel had been very welcome when he was around because the pair of them would stay up drinking whilst Rachel and her father had long given up and gone to bed.

No, it was ok by Rachel that her father wasn't at her mother's funeral. Steve was going to have to deal with that in his own way. Rachel could no longer be disappointed by her father's actions or lack of them because she no longer had any expectations. Steve, on the other hand, perhaps because he was a father himself, who had recently separated from his wife, expected his dad to support his children at this emotional time and pay his final respects to the woman who might not have been his ideal wife, but who raised his two children pretty much single-handedly and did a fantastic job of it.

And yet, Rachel had been constantly disappointed in her own mother. She had consistently fallen short of her expectations, feelings which had been compounded when Rachel became a mother herself. She couldn't fathom the powerful feelings of unconditional love she had for her own children with the conditional love she had received from her own mother. Perhaps daughters don't forgive their mothers as they forgive their fathers, because they will never be a father. The same might be true in reverse for sons.

None of these thoughts were helping Rachel get through the wake. What did any of it matter now? Her mother was dead. Nothing could change the past, there were no more words that could be said, no more hands to hold or hugs to be shared. Feeling regret at a funeral was a futile exercise. Death had had its last word, the finality of death leaves the bereaved with a full stop they have no control over.

There was no point in being angry with her step mother or her father. Nothing she could do or say would change the situation. Nothing she could do or say would suddenly remove the divide or compensate for the years of distance. Steve's anger wasn't going to make their father change his mind. It just served to make him feel angry with no-one to be angry at. If their father did feel guilt, he certainly hadn't adjusted his behaviour to atone for it. He'd continued through life as he always had: a positive optimist who's mood remained the same from one year to the next or a deluded spineless fool who allowed himself to be controlled. It depended how you looked at it.

She sat down heavily in the corner of the pub and decided to enjoy the company of people who reminded her of happy times during her childhood. People who had fond memories of her mother and were delighted to be sharing them with her now. Eddie was taking care of the kids and Rachel was free to chat amongst adults, telling them about her life now and learning about the lives of their grown-up children.

"Your mum was beautiful."

"She was a fearsome woman."

"I fancied her, but she wouldn't give me house room." Was the final comment that stuck in Rachel's head. Yes, her mum was a woman. Men fancied her. Women were friends with her and people admired her. She might not have been the winner of mother of the year, but she did do a good job of bringing her kids up and she did provide a good home for them. Rachel hoped her own kids would be happy hearing and feeling those things about her when she died.

"It was a good send off," said Gordon, Rachel's step dad.

"Yeah, she'd have been happy with that." Replied Steve.

"We'll drive you back Gordon and make sure you're ok." Eddie's offer was eagerly accepted by Gordon and they made their way to car.

"Thanks for dropping me off and being there for me Rachel." There'd been a pause in the conversation and Gordon filled it with the first thing he could think of.

"It's ok, Gordon. Thanks for looking after mum and being there for us. We couldn't have managed without you." It's true, Rachel could not have managed her mother's illness from two hundred miles away. Gordon had been a life-saver in that respect.

"Will you be ok if we head off?" Asked Rachel.

"Yeah, I want some time on my own anyway." Gordon looked weary.

"Right, well we'll be off then."

"Ok, see you soon."

As Rachel and her family pulled away from the house, her heart broke. The strength she'd been holding onto crumbled with each heaving sob she left her mother further and further behind. Her own daughter's hand crept round her shoulder from the back seat of the car.

"Mum, it's ok," she said. "Grandma would have enjoyed today. She had the funeral she wanted."

"Thanks love. I love you all." Rachel patted Eddie's knee.

"Love you too mum." That's what kept Rachel going. Her children and her husband with the unconditional love they all had for each other.

This was how she had imagined her life being. Nothing could prevent her from having the family life she deserved. Rachel had made sure of that.

Day Eight - The Businessman
21st December

Luckily, Rachel's client wasn't due until later in the afternoon. The kids were being picked up by Eddie from their various activities and Rachel had managed to rest throughout the day so she could listen carefully to her client's woes.

Her practice was well balanced between men and women. Most people assumed it was mainly bored housewives and uptight career women who saw Rachel, but this was not the case. Men appeared as frequently and their problems were no greater and no less than those of the women. The way they behaved was different. Very different. Anger was a common theme. Rachel observed that whilst women seemed to take their problems out on themselves, men seemed to be angry with those around them. All of the people she worked with consoled themselves with a range of sometimes bizarre peccadillos ranging from odd sexual fantasies to full blown addictions.

This client was a workaholic. He'd been seeking help from Rachel for six months and had appeared because of the break-down of his marriage. Rachel quite liked Phil. He was straight forward, down to earth and had a decent sense of humour. He was also evasive on just about every subject Rachel could think of. She wanted some kind of break-through for him before the Christmas holidays and before she took a few months off on maternity leave. She was hoping today would bring things to a head for Phil and allow her to experience a degree of job satisfaction.

Phil knew the routine and was already sitting comfortably in the usual spot, waiting for Rachel to take her place.

"How are you today?" She enquired lightly

"Good Rachel. How about you?" One of Phil's tactics was to ask her questions so he could avoid answering hers. She'd been caught out once or twice, sharing perhaps a little too much of her own history than she thought was professional. Phil was charming. In his youth, he was probably quite good looking and what he lacked in looks, he made up for in a winning smile, a certain gentlemanly gallantry and good old fashioned flirtatious charm. When she first met Phil, she'd found herself wondering what he'd be like in bed. This had been quite distracting during their first therapy session and Rachel was thankful that her swollen belly was a powerful deterrent for her amorous thoughts and she suspected Phil's too.

She'd never have cheated on Eddie, but the thoughts were strong enough to have concerned her at the time.

"I'm good too, Phil. Let's look at where we left off last time. I felt you were making progress, don't you?" She paused, waiting for Phil to gather his thoughts. This often took longer than most clients. He needed plenty of time to work out the best way of saying things. Rachel knew he was dyslexic and she assumed the silences were necessary for Phil to get his ideas in the best order.

She waited.

Phil started to speak, then stopped himself. For a moment he closed his eyes and Rachel grabbed the pause to glance out of the window into her beautiful garden. There were chaffinches on the bird feeders, scrapping, chatting and dropping the husks of their grain on the damp soil below the tree. Those would sprout in the spring, thought Rachel and I'll be picking the weeds out of the ground before you know it.

"I married the wrong woman." This was a very matter of fact statement from Phil and was the first time he'd said anything negative about his estranged wife.

"Ok, do you want to tell me a bit more about that statement?" Asked Rachel.

"Diane was a fantastic mother. Our two kids are great. She did a great job."

"Good" said Rachel, "go on."

"She never understood me. She doesn't understand my business. We didn't talk about anything that I was interested in." Phil was finding the words he needed much more readily than he had in previous sessions.

"Ok Phil, it sounds as though there's quite a lot in that short sentence. Would it be helpful to explain it in more detail to me?" She sensed that Phil was more than ready to get a few things off his chest.

"Yeah. It would."

"Good stuff. I'm listening. I'll only stop you if I feel you're heading down a path that's not leading anywhere useful or repeating things over again which don't appear to be moving your thinking forward. Is that ok?"

"Yes. That's fine." Replied Phil.

"Tell me about how you met Diane. What was she like?"

"We met in my home town. She worked as a junior in the hairdressers and I used to get my haircut there. I'm older than her and I always fancied her. All the local lads fancied her. She was in demand, but never agreed to go out with any of them. I'm not sure if any of them actually had the balls to ask her out. She seemed so out of our league. Beautiful, long wavy hair, stunning body and those piercing green eyes. I played it cool with her. I didn't want her to know I was one of the many admirers she had. I kept her guessing. You need to coax beautiful women. They don't just come to you when you ask. You have to be patient and play the long game.

Rachel suppressed a wry smile. Phil's charm, combined with his nineteen seventies attitudes towards women were often endearing.

"When she turned eighteen, I asked her out and she said, 'yes'. We've been together ever since. "

"I started my business about five years after we got married. We had two kids really quickly and they were just at primary school when I got my business off the ground. I worked all the hours God sent. I worked weekends, evening, nights, holidays, Christmas, the kids birthdays, Diane's birthdays, anniversaries, everything. I missed everything. I didn't see a single sports day, nativity play, concert, football match. I didn't do homework with the kids. Nothing. Diane did it all. She was a single parent. I paid the bills.

I bought her a bigger and bigger house every time the business grew. I took her to fancier restaurants and bought her nice clothes. She didn't want for anything. Her friends were always jealous of what she had. We'd move to the show home on exclusive housing estates, buying all the fixtures and fittings. We had the latest TV, the newest cars and were the first to have a hot tub in the garden.

"I made sure she wasn't lonely. I got babysitters in so she could go out when I was working and I paid for them to go on holiday when I couldn't. When I could get away, we went with friends so Diane had some company. I took care of everything. And all I wanted in return was a bit of appreciation. A thank you every now and then. A kiss, a cuddle, stuff I'd ask for in the bedroom to be provided. She had to look neat. I don't like any of that messy *can't be bothered stuff* that some wives think is acceptable. Diane always did me proud. She always looked the part. I'd help her choose the right dress for the right occasion and help her out in restaurants so she knew what she was ordering. She needed that kind of guidance from me in the early days and just got used to me taking care of everything.

"When the kids left home, I even found a job for her in the business. We kept it professional, never talked about home life at work and never ever discussed business at home. I didn't tell her anything about the business. There was no point. She wouldn't have understood anyway.

"And now she wants half my fucking money."

Rachel raised her eyebrows ever so slightly. She'd never heard Phil swear before. She hoped he hadn't noticed. She didn't want to think he was being judged.

He carried on. He hadn't noticed.

"My son won't speak to me because he thinks I've been a cunt to his mother. I've given her everything and him. The only person who understands me is my daughter. She's at uni studying business studies and she knows what it's all about. I never thought my daughter would be smarter than my son. I tried to get my son interested in the business, I even bought him a bloody iMac for Christmas and an Apple Watch. Technology is the future you know, it's everything and all he's bloody interested in is his art. He sits about all day painting and drawing. What use is that to anyone? His girlfriend works so he can play the arty farty type at home. He cooks her dinner every night. It's pathetic. What kind of man does that? I'm thinking of getting Isobel into the business full time after she graduates, she's much smarter than Jake."

There was too much for Rachel to contend with in this flow of disappointment. She didn't quite know where to begin. How could this man have grown up in the Twentieth century with views which belonged in the nineteenth.

"I'm disappointed with Jake."

Rachel's thoughts were often mirrored by her client's words and it had long ago ceased to freak her out, she accepted it now as part of the rapport she and her clients built between each other.

"What about Isobel? Are you disappointed with her too?"

"No, but she's bound to let me down at some point. Everyone does. You can't trust anyone. Even your family."

"That sounds quite final. Everyone let's you down? Everyone?" Rachel wanted Phil to consider his sweeping generalisation carefully. Where was the hope, the love, the trust and what kind of future would Phil have without believing that not everyone would let you down.

"Yes. Everyone. You can't trust anyone. Except my mother. I trusted her. She was always there for me."

It always came back to the mother. Good, bad, indifferent, absent, present, rich, poor, kind, mean, working, a housewife: it didn't matter. The mother was always there, forming, shaping, guiding, mis-guiding and loving or neglecting. She was always the back drop to her client's lives.

"What about your father?" Father's weren't absent from therapy, they just didn't seem to get the same amount of air-time.

"He left me and my mother when I was six. He moved us half way across the world and left after six months. We'd had a fantastic life in America. A big house, pool, big car and more money that we knew what to do with. My dad was a sales rep and seemed to be doing well, but for some reason that has never been explained to me, we moved to shitey wee village on the East Coast of Scotland and my life changed forever. My mum had to go out to work. I was bullied by the kids at school because I had a funny accent and I never fitted in. It was just me and my mum. She was always there for me and now I'm there for her." Phil looked out at the garden with a softer expression on his face than Rachel had seen so far in their sessions. She thought he looked like a lost school boy. Very vulnerable, very alone. In a nano-second, the look disappeared and the hard jaw with the resolute mouth and unblinking eyes returned.

"She can't live forever. Why is she dying and why is my dad still fit and healthy? Why is she leaving me instead of my dad?" These were rhetorical questions.

"I don't know Phil." Rachel didn't have any answers for him. It was often the most cherished, loved and cared for people who went before the ones you would like to see the back of died. She knew that from her personal experience.

"What are your thoughts about the new year Phil? There's an opportunity to make a fresh start this year, what would you like to focus on? What would you like more of in your life?" Rachel wanted Phil out of his gloom and consider the possibility of light.

"More of the same. I've got the business. I can't leave that. No one can do their job without me. The place would fall apart if I wasn't there. I have to keep an eye on everyone. I've got cameras so I can check up on people when I'm not there, but there's no substitute for me being there and monitoring everyone. If there were more people like me in the business, it would be easy, but there aren't so I have to be there."

Rachel had heard this diatribe on more than one occasion from Phil and had been unable to open him up to the possibility that there were very capable people in his business and that leaving them to get on with things was probably a great way to improve their skills and give him a much needed break. Phil had returned to his fixed belief that he couldn't trust anyone and so spending time away from the business wasn't on the agenda for the new year or any year for that matter.

Rachel tried a new tack. "How about the long term future? What are your plans for the next ten years?"

"I have to build the business so it's big enough to sell."

"Great, how much money do you want from the business to give you the lifestyle you want?"

"I don't know." Rachel was surprised, she thought Phil would probably have a figure in mind.

"Well, how much is enough?"

"I don't know. What is enough? I want to feel secure and I don't know how much money will give me that feeling? It's why I can't stop working. It's why I don't go on holiday for more than a week at a time. It's why I don't have a relationship with my son and why my wife finally left me. If I knew the answer, I wouldn't be here."

"What kind of things would you like to be doing instead of working?" Asked Rachel.

"I have to be doing something. I get bored sitting about doing nothing. When Diane and I went on holiday, she'd lie by the pool and I'd have to go out and do something. I can't sit still. I'd prefer to be working."

There were times in therapy when Rachel knew that no progress would be made until something major shifted in the lives of her clients. Like Joyce and her friend's funeral, Phil needed an event, maybe a health scare, maybe an accident, something that would help him notice what was really important in life. She knew there were people too who were a little too close to the psychopath scale than she cared to admit. Phil was not an emotional desert, so she'd discounted that, but he really didn't understand that people had feelings or emotional needs. He hadn't noticed that his wife wanted affection, not bigger and bigger houses. He hadn't noticed that his son wanted his father's approval, not the latest tech gadget. Phil really didn't seem to be able to grasp the emotional needs of those people around him. Rachel shuddered to think what he was like at work. She knew he fired people on a regular basis and only had his side of the story about their supposed levels of incompetence. His comments about everything being easier if people were more like him was definitely an indication of poor emotional intelligence.

She felt sorry for him. He'd worked so hard all his life, providing financial security for himself, his family and his employees and he felt they'd all let him down in one way or another. He felt lonely and unappreciated and yet hadn't realised that the satisfaction and security he was looking for, was inside of him.

"I'm wondering," Rachel began, "because you can't name a sum of money that will make you feel secure, can you begin to feel secure right now, inside. If you were to feel secure, where in your body would you feel it?"

Phil frowned hard, his face wrinkled and creased whilst his brain processed the question.

"My stomach." Phil patted his stomach.

"Good, if you were to know, what colour would that feeling of security be?"

"Blue."

"Ok, can you spread that feeling throughout your body, increasing those levels of security."

Phil sat back and closed his eyes. For the first time in the six months Rachel had been working with him, he had begun to look relaxed. Maybe, progress had finally been made.

She gave him a few more moments and then she said, "Ok, Phil tell me how you feel now."

"Ok. I feel ok now, but I know as soon as I get back to the office, I'll feel the same as I did this morning before I saw you."

Rachel smiled to hide her disappointment.

"What would it take to get that feeling more of the time?" She asked, really hoping that Phil would find some degree of peace in his life. She hated to think of his constant disappointment in everyone and everything around him. It can't have been nice being married to or working with someone for whom you knew you would constantly fall short of their expectations. Phil's favourite word was disappointment. It was one of the first things Rachel had noticed about him.

"I'd have to live on an island on my own in the middle of nowhere. People will always let you down, it's just the way they are."

"Do you fall short of your own expectations of yourself Phil?" People often transferred their own failings onto the people around them. This was worth a shot.

"No. I'm not perfect, I know that, but no one can meet my standards."

Rachel immediately stopped feeling sorry for Phil. His last few words had rung a large alarm bell in her head. There was a very fine line between high standards and control freakery that bordered on abuse. Rachel suddenly saw her ex-husband standing over her, criticising her attempts to varnish the bedside table, his comments about her cooking, his disdain for her clothes, how she wore them, when she wore them and who saw her in them. She knew she wouldn't be able to work with Phil again. He was simply too sure he was right. She couldn't help someone who lacked that much self-doubt.

She didn't blame Phil's son for rejecting his father and almost asked Phil if Jake wanted to see her for an appointment at one stage. She felt desperately sorry for his wife. The poor woman was probably an under-confident wreck. Rachel hoped that his daughter was robust enough to withstand her father's over-critical and judgemental eye that he felt duty bound to place on everyone. He paid for everything and everyone, which in his mind gave him permission to control. He wasn't going to let that go in a hurry any time soon. He would grow his business and bring more people into control, he would see his estranged wife financially secure and still control her through money and those he couldn't control, he would sack, ignore or write out of his life completely.

Rachel was frustrated and annoyed with herself that at the beginning of Phil's therapy sessions, she had been charmed by him. She could see how persuasive he had been. She had almost been drawn into his way of thinking. She fell back on her training for solace and made her decision.

"Well Phil, I think we've come to the end of the road. I'm not sure there's anymore I can do for you. You seem to be content in your way of thinking and aren't prepared to change it. We will make this the last session, if that's ok with you Phil."

"Yes. It's fine with me. I didn't think anyone could help me anyway. People promise so much don't they and they never deliver. I have an office full of people who lied at interview about how great they were and none of them deliver. It's just the way things are. Thanks for trying to help me Rachel. I appreciate it." He seemed genuine in his thanks. There was the charm returning, making Rachel feel temporarily guilty about dismissing this lonely man.

"The last thing I'll say to you Phil is this: they're only the way they are because that's what you believe. If you believe people are doing their best with good intentions and can be trusted, until they demonstrate otherwise, then that's what you'll experience. The world will seem like a less lonely place and people will be much more appreciative."

Phil took out his wad of cash and paid Rachel her consultancy fee, shrugging his shoulders and giving her a disbelieving look.

"We'll see," he said as he walked down the path, "we'll see."

Maybe Phil had seen through Rachel. You never really know people, even people you are married to. A vague recollection of a statistic popped into Rachel's head: you only really know five percent of a person because you cannot read their mind. Your thoughts are your own. Ideas that you have may come and go and no one knows about them unless you put them into action.

Had Phil seen through Rachel's demeanour, he would have seen the secrets she kept, just like everyone else. Maybe that was why he was permanently disappointed. He couldn't control those thoughts and he didn't have a handle on the secrets in people's heads. It was the only thing he couldn't control and it frustrated him enormously.

Rachel understood and empathised to a degree with his frustration. It would be easy to become bitter and disappointed in human beings and yet Rachel chose hope. She preferred to see people doing their best and attempting to make a life for themselves with the resources they had available to them.

It was too easy to allow darkness to overcome you. She preferred light, although it was often harder to find, particularly in her chosen profession. She found solace in her children and in the love she shared with Eddie. At times, her family felt like her saving grace. What would be Phil's saving grace now his family were distancing themselves from him? He would work harder and harder until he dropped. His idea that security could be found in money was leading him to a lonely grave. Ideas, beliefs, whatever you want to call them, have consequences, particularly when you turn them into reality. Rachel understood this all too well.

Day Nine - The Third Wife

22nd December

When Rachel woke up, she counted the days once again until the due date of her baby. Not long to go now. The baby could come anytime soon and it would be healthy. There were a few loose ends for Rachel to tidy up around her therapy practice and Christmas chores, then she could relax.

Her client today was a referral from someone she'd worked with many years previously. This happened with a fair amount of frequency and Rachel was pleased that she didn't have to advertise and promote her practice as much as she had in the beginning. She made a decent living now, but in the early days of her practice, she'd been very short of cash. Her training alone had cost thousands of pounds, an investment she felt had been well worthwhile.

The change in her career had been necessary for her sanity. Ten years in a relationship with an addict had required much soul searching and that had led to a career in helping people like herself get over their own personal histories. Not everyone had dark secrets like Rachel, or none they were prepared to admit to her, but the people she met had a wide range of traumas, trials and tribulations to overcome.

Most people came to her wondering if they were normal. She told them there was no such thing as normal. People deal with things in different ways and some people simply found it harder than others to cope with life's ups and downs. In her experience, there were very few people who sailed through life without any issues and if they claimed to be, then they were probably lying or a psychopath who didn't have any feelings to hurt.

The lady who stood on Rachel's front door step today looked bright and breezy. In the way that women over fifty suddenly decide blonde is their natural hair colour, this lady had highlighted hair. It was over highlighted and very dry, almost straw-like in its condition. She had a slight hump in her shoulders and stood looking up at Rachel through sun glasses, she had a broad smile. She wore expensive looking flat bright blue shoes and sandy coloured trousers, her top was patterned with gaudy flowers, reminding Rachel of the tops you find in those trendy looking shops in Spain.

"Hello. Lovely to meet you. Please come in." Rachel greeted her new client with an equally broad smile.

"Hi, I'm Sam. You must be Rachel." Sam put her long, thin, slightly withered arm out to shake Rachel's hand. It shook ever so slightly adding to the sense of fragility.

"Please. Come through."

The two women passed through the house into the garden. No rain today, just a bright, clear, cold, crisp day. They type of winter day that Rachel loved. She adored the smell of the air when it was cold and clear. She breathed in the freshness of the day and detected the delicate decay of leaves slowly disintegrating in to mulch which would be useful for next year's flowers. The apple trees which were trained against the garden wall, appreciated the goodness of the dead leaves, providing sweet tasting apples each autumn.

"Beautiful day, isn't it?" Rachel enquired, not really expecting an answer.

"Yes, beautiful." Sam's voice sounded much more confident than her client's usually sounded and contradicted the sense of decay that her shaky, withered arm had portrayed.

Sam accepted a strong black coffee without sugar and sat very upright in the chair, or as upright as her stopped shoulders would allow. She looked directly at Rachel in an expectant manner.

"Tell me about what's brought you here today Sam." Rachel got the impression that a very forthright approach was required today.

"I'm here on behalf of my husband." It was common for clients to present their own issues as those of their loved ones. It's not me, it's them,' was a common starting point in therapy.

"Ok. I can't work with someone unless they want to be here Sam. If you want me to work with your husband, you need to ask him to contact me directly and arrange an appointment for himself." Rachel could still charge full price for the session even if ended there and then. Her cancellation terms were very clear on her website and she always re-issued them when the appointment was confirmed via email.

"Yes, I'm happy for you to work with him, but I'm here to tell you about him so you understand what you'll be dealing with." She was very matter of fact.

"If you want to talk to me about your relationship with your husband, then I'm happy to listen. I won't be asking you questions about him though, I'll only ask you about you Sam. As long as we have that understanding, I am prepared to listen. I would only accept your husband as a client if he called me and personally asked me for an appointment." Rachel felt it was well worthwhile repeating this as she suspected Sam hadn't heard her the first time.

"Yes, yes. I get that. I know I don't need any therapy, I've been very happy for a long time, my life is fantastic since we moved to the Highlands. It really is the best decision we've made in thirty five years. I love the people and we've settled in so well. We have a better social life there than we've ever had and it's a real mixture of nationalities where we live. People seem to be drawn to Applecross from all over the world."

Rachel knew vaguely where Applecross was. She'd seen it on a map and it stuck out on the far west coast of Scotland. There was one road in and one road out. It was supposed to be stunning, a real gem, sitting on the banks of a sea loch, peppered with small inlets and islands, surrounded by hills. It was often cut off in the winter, but like most remote places, she suspected the residents quite liked the resilient attitude they shared amongst each other. That and large chest freezers they kept well stocked.

"We had a house built there three years ago when we both retired. Our daughter was finally settled with her husband and with no sign of grandchildren on the horizon so we decided to sell up, clear the last remnants of the mortgage and live in a field in the middle of nowhere. There's a thriving community of amateur dramatists and I find myself as director of the latest production. We've joined the historical society and there are so many festivals, we're always involved in something. It's quite fantastic. As I say, it's the best decision we've ever made."

She hardly paused for breath as she described the idyllic lifestyle, her spindly arms waving in broad, grand gestures. Rachel could imagine Sam directing the local am-drams, gesticulating in a similar fashion. She wasn't sure whether she personally could stand someone so confident and directive, but luckily she didn't have to live in Applecross or partake in am-dram activities with people like Sam.

"It sounds like you have got life pretty much sorted, I'm not sure how you want me to help." Sam hoped she'd masked the frustration in her voice, bordering on annoyance. She often wanted to give her clients a shake to wake them up from their self-indulgent issues. People like Joyce had problems, even Stephanie had her issues, but she was struggling to see how Sam's situation had led her to her office in the garden.

"It's my step children."

"Ok, what about them?"

"I detest them." Sam's faced contorted, her mouth tightening, her lips thinning into a grimace as the words came out of her mouth.

"They're always in the background. Always to be considered. I've had to share my husband with them for almost forty years and I want them to leave us alone. I persuaded Graham to move to the Highlands because it was particularly hard to get there. Graham's son had started visiting us when he travelled for business before we moved and I couldn't stand the thought of him being able to pop in whenever he wanted. As for Graham's daughter, I can't stand being in the same room as her."

Rachel could tell Sam wasn't going to stop her vent. She made an attempt to interrupt, but failed and Sam continued.

"That bitch, Graham's first wife never thought I was good enough to look after he precious children when they came to visit at weekends. She'd insisted on inspecting my house and my bloody kitchen cupboards before she allowed her little darlings to stay. I've never been so humiliated in all my life."

Rachel managed to ask, "How long ago was this Sam?"

"Oh, when they were six and nine, which must have been ... hmmm" she looked up to make sure she had calculated correctly, "almost forty years ago."

"I am sensing a strong feeling of bitterness Sam, which doesn't appear to have rescinded."

"Of course I feel bitter. Who wouldn't feel that way? Graham's children both have children of their own, although I was quite pleased that both their first marriages failed. They'd got married in their twenties and were so smug in their neat little lives, living in nice homes in the countryside. Graham wouldn't stop going on and on about how proud he was of them and how happy he was that they were settled with their respective spouses. God, it made me sick, he never said anything like that to me about my work or my achievements.

Our daughter, Sarah, doesn't have any children. She's married now, which I'm very happy about, but I can't help but feel she could have done better for herself. I had so many high hopes for Sarah. We put her through a very expensive school to give her every chance possible to do well in life. We were upset when she failed to get into Oxford, but were happy enough with St Andrews. I thought she'd get a job in the City or the Civil Service, but she didn't." Sam's voice trailed off as she looked down to floor, her flood of vitriol slowing down to a trickle.

"Would you say Sarah is happy though?"

"Yes, she seems happy enough."

"I am not sure what you have to be bitter about Sam?"

"We have a bloody lunch between Christmas and New Year that Graham's kids and grandchildren insist on coming to every year. He looks forward to it and I thought it would come to an end when we moved, but it's worse because they stay for a few days now and there's nothing I can do. I have to sit there and listen to how fantastic their lives are, what brilliant work they're doing and how amazing their businesses are. It makes me sick. I'm not interested in their lives, why on earth would I be interested in them or their pathetic children?"

"That seems quite a harsh way of looking at things, don't you think?" Enquired Rachel.

"No, we spent a fortune on Sarah's education and all Graham's grandchildren went to state school, despite him encouraging his children to send them to private schools. They seem to have done quite well and they have a bloody opinion about everything. I brought Sarah up to listen to me and follow my guidance like a good daughter ought to. Graham's grandchildren and his children don't listen to a word I say and they have the audacity to disagree with me in front of Graham. He doesn't do a thing to defend me. It's ridiculous. I'm his wife. He should agree with me, not them."

Rachel wondered how someone could become so self-centred and bitter, a little light bulb lit up in her brain as she remembered the slight tremor in Sam's handshake and she asked, "How much do you drink Sam?"

"What's that got to do with anything? Her hackles went up, her entire body went rigid and she glared at Rachel. Then Rachel noticed the plethora of threads veins across Sam's cheeks and nose. The tremor in her hand as she moved them around as she spoke. Her thin, skeletal frame with a large round belly and her bloodshot eyes. Rachel had put the bloodshot eyes down to fatigue, but she was now wondering whether it was alcohol abuse that was causing the disfiguration both physically and emotionally. Sam's face showed signs of puffiness, which could have been due to late nights or alcohol abuse.

"I'm like anyone these days, I have a g&t before dinner and then a bottle of wine with my meal. It's all perfectly sociable. I don't need to drink: I enjoy it." The defensiveness was still in Sam's voice.

"Ok, Sam, you're going to have to help me understand what's driving the bitterness and resentment you feel against your step children. They're no threat to you. They don't appear to need financial support from you or Graham. What's at the heart of your feelings?" Rachel chose the word heart on purpose, so far she hadn't experienced much heart in Sam and wanted to get her to think about love.

"He's bloody changed his will again." Her anger was palpable.

"When Sarah graduated and she moved into the flat we bought her, I persuaded Graham to change his will. It seemed sensible to me that if he died first, all his property and money ought to go to me and then I would obviously leave it all to Sarah. I was worried that if he died first he would inherit my wealth and then distribute it evenly between his three children. I don't want my hard earned money going to someone else's offspring, particularly the offspring of a woman I detested. In my opinion, it's fairer for Sarah to inherit everything and then she can split it between her half siblings if she so wishes. They're pretty well off as far as I can tell and Sarah doesn't earn that much in her call centre role. She's a team leader, but I don't suppose that pays much. Her husband doesn't earn that much either. They need the money more than Graham's kids do."

"Ok". Rachel was trying to put herself in the shoes of Sam, the shoes of Graham's kids and consider the situation from Graham's point of view. She felt sorry for him. He was either going to feel the wrath of his wife or the children from his first marriage. He wasn't in a good position, whatever way you looked at it.

"He's changed his will so that if I die first and he inherits everything, then when he dies, it is divided equally between his kids."

"That doesn't sound too unreasonable Sam. You'll be financially secure if he dies first won't you. Sarah and her husband will still be ok too."

Sam hadn't heard Rachel's comments and she carried on ranting, "I knew I shouldn't have let his children talk to him at lunch. Somehow, they'd managed to sit next to him at the other end of the table and have a private conversation with him. I'd made sure for years that they weren't alone together because I knew something like this would happen. He's so weak you see. I rarely let him go out on his own, but he must have used the excuse of buying my Christmas present because that's the only time I can think of when he was alone. He won't tell me which solicitor he's used either. I've checked with our usual one and they won't tell me anything. It's so bloody annoying. For all these years I've managed his relationship with his kids in a very satisfactory manner. He saw just about enough of them to satisfy his need to be a proper father, but not too much that he could get too close. I never invited them to stay at our house and if they came I made sure we had something planned so they couldn't stay too long. It's easy to make people feel uncomfortable in your home if you know how."

Rachel really didn't like this woman. If things hadn't turned out the way they had in her life with her ex-husband, her own children could quite easily have been subjected to a step-mother like Sam. Luckily, her ex-husband was no longer a problem she needed to worry about.

"What will you do?"

"I'll need to outlive Graham or convince him to change his will back to the way it was. He takes tablets for his blood pressure and his diabetes, maybe I'll forget to remind him to take his tablets or maybe I'll add a little more salt to his meals and encourage him to eat a few more potatoes."

"Sam, may I remind you of my duty as a therapist: I am legally obliged to report to the relevant authorities any matters where I feel harm will be done against the individual or other individuals or where laws are being broken." Rachel sounded very stern. She wanted Sam to realise what she was saying.

Plotting to kill your spouse, whether that was by omission or not, was still plotting to kill your spouse. Rachel considered this notion and was on the very edge of an open admission of her own, when she stopped herself in her tracks. She drew a deep breath, holding the words in, remembering that sometimes a therapist could share too much of their own experience with their clients. This near miss, scared Rachel. Had Sam been a more appealing human being, someone who was easier to like and warm to, would Rachel have revealed her own failings. She had to have more control. She must bury those thoughts deeper. Lock them away for ever.

Fortunately for Rachel, the moment passed and her self-absorbed client continued with her monologue.

"Oh, don't be silly. I was only joking. I wouldn't harm Graham. What would I do in Applecross all by myself. No, I love him dearly and will simply have to live with his decision. I just need to stay healthy. My Dr says that despite the falls I've had in the last few years I'm an absolute picture of health."

"Falls?"

"Yes, I fell down the stairs and broke my ankle a few years ago. It's full of pins you know. Then I fell over backwards and smashed my skull on a radiator, that has a titanium plate in it now. I was stone cold sober on both occasions. I hadn't been drinking at all." Rachel knew this must be a lie. Why repeat the assertion that she was sober. In her experience, people only did that when they were convincing themselves of the truth.

"Then there was that health scare when I thought I had skin cancer. I'd told Graham and the family that I had cancer and of course, I thought it was true myself for a while. Luckily the biopsy came back benign."

"That must have been a relief to everyone concerned." Rachel lied

"Well, this was about ten years ago and they all thought I'd made a miraculous recovery. The truth was I didn't tell them it was benign for seven years. It was my little secret you see." The smirk across Sam's face underlined her smug tones.

"You didn't tell your husband it was benign and you let him think you'd had skin cancer for seven years?" Rachel did not hide the incredulity in her voice.

"Yes, of course. It did him no harm. It made no difference to him, I was still alive and well. Besides, he became even more biddable. That's how I managed to get him to move. We all manipulate the truth to get what we want Rachel. Don't pretend you're better than me or anyone else for that matter. Us women have little power as it is, we need to be smarter than the men to get what we want. Don't you think?"

Rachel did not like the table being turned on her. She asked the questions, not her clients. She shifted uncomfortably in her chair and hoped her poker face hid her true feelings and thoughts. She knew she was guilty of lying to get what she wanted, but she wasn't about the share any of her secrets with this woman, her nano-second of weakness was now passed. She glanced at the clock on the wall, hoping the time for Sam's session was close.

"I think there are lies we can tell that hurt people and lies we can tell that avoid hurting people and actually protect people. I prefer to stick to the latter kind of lie. That's how I live my life Sam."

"No one was hurt by my lie were they? What can someone say, 'it's a shame you didn't have cancer?' That would make them look rather callous wouldn't it? No, Graham couldn't react in the face of my tears. He really can't stand my weepy moments. He forgives anything once I turn on the waterworks." Sam flashed a broad smile at Rachel. It reminded her of her first experience of Shakespeare at the theatre when she saw Lady Macbeth persuading her hapless husband to commit murder.

"Would you say your drinking was under control Sam?" Rachel insisted on pressing this point once again. She recognised so many of the signs of alcohol abuse because she'd lived with an alcoholic for ten years. Their level of manipulation was astounding. Her ex-husband had shown an outward face of generosity, kindness and caring to friends and family in the same way that Sam appeared to describe. She wasn't short of friends and seemed to have had a decent career. People were clearly taken in by her outgoing nature and her ability to make people feel at ease in her company in just the same way that Rachel's ex-husband had been able to do.

'He's such a great guy your husband.' 'He's so good with the children, you're so lucky to have a man like that.' Rachel had heard these things over the years from other mums and her own mother. She'd even convinced herself that this was true. There weren't many men who would stay at home with young children whilst his wife built her business. He had cooked her dinner every night whilst she bathed the kids. Without the large quantities of vodka mixed with his orange juice, their marriage might have been perfect. Nothing was ever perfect though. No one heard him tell her that she wasn't allowed to leave the house because if she did, he would drink. No, one knew about his ability to change from a happy go luck man into a dark moody man with no warning. No one knew about the crockery he threw, the vile words he used to described Rachel's degrees of uselessness or the lies he told to hide his drinking habit.

Nothing was ever his fault, just as nothing seemed to be Sam's fault.

"Look, Rachel, I didn't come here to talk about my social habits, I came here to unburden myself of the injustices that are going on in my life. Have you any idea what it's like to live with a spineless jelly fish? He couldn't stand up to his first two wives and he can't stand up to his children now." Sam's false smile had changed rapidly into a twisted grimace. Her hackles were well and truly up now, her finger pointing aggressively at Rachel as she spat the words out.

"Have you considered leaving him?" This was the only tack left for Rachel to take. She was close to kicking Sam out of her office.

"Don't be ridiculous! I couldn't bear to be on my own. No, I need Graham there. I have a terrible fear of the dark and find it almost impossible to sleep alone at night. He's my rock."

So, she did love him, or at least needed him, thought Rachel.

"What is it about the dark that frightens you Sam?" Rachel found her soft therapist's voice once again.

"My mother used to scrub me down in the bath with washing powder when she thought I'd been lying to her. She would tuck me up in bed and tell me stories about the serial killer who was found hanging in the attic of the house we used to live in and then she'd tell me to pray to the Virgin Mary because she was the only one who could save me."

Sam described this disturbing scene in a very matter of fact way. There wasn't a glimmer of emotion on display.

"How old were you when this happened?"

"Oh, it happened from a very early age right up until I left home at eighteen. My first husband used to make it worse. He would deliberately jump out from behind the door in our bedroom at night as a I came up the stairs. In the end, I had to sleep downstairs as I was too terrified to visit our bedroom." There was still no evidence of emotion on Sam's face.

Was she shutting down wondered Rachel or did she really not feel anything anymore. Rachel had in the recent passed blocked out certain memories from her own filing cabinet of life. She'd learned techniques which helped her to wipe her dirty slate clean. Had Sam been able to do the same?

"When I left him I had to move to a house with a downstairs bathroom, it was only when I met Graham that I was able to sleep upstairs. There are so many things I'm grateful to him for. When I'm with him, I'm not afraid of anything. When he was away on business, the only way I could sleep was to take two sleeping tablets and drink several large g&t's." Finally, Sam looked vulnerable and small. Her stoop seemingly more pronounced and her skeletal frame positioned awkwardly against the chair.

For the first time, Rachel noticed how small Sam actually was. Not only was she bony, but she was fragile too. Her thin arms hung like those of a rag doll from her scrawny shoulders. The stooped back was very narrow and her trousers covered tiny, spindly legs. Rachel saw the frightened child for the first time. She couldn't imagine what it was like to be scared half to death by your own mother. Neither could she understand what it felt like to be viciously scrubbed down in the bath with harsh, caustic soap powder as a small, defenceless child. These days it would be counted as abuse. In Sam's day it was considered to be good discipline.

"Would you say you drink to mask your feelings Sam?" As she asked this question, Rachel felt a thunder bolt strike in her mind. She'd never considered this as a reason for drinking. Was this why her ex-husband had drunk to excess?

"I like to drink because it makes me feel powerful. It's important to me that I'm in control. That's why Graham and I have lasted for such a long time, he knows I'm the boss and he knows he must do as he is told. People listen to me when I drink and I don't see that as a problem. I could stop tomorrow if I wanted to." Her voice was defiant with no hint of compromise.

"Have you tried to stop?" Asked Rachel.

"No, I don't need to. Why would I stop something that's perfectly normal."

Personal and professional experience had taught Rachel that without an admission of a problem, there would be no solution. She needed to bring the session to a close, but she wasn't sure what Sam had hoped to achieve. Her complaints had been contradictory: one minute she described her husband as a jelly fish and the next he was the perfect partner who understood her past. Was Rachel just someone else Sam could manipulate, lie to and charm?

This circular conversation went round several times in Rachel's head, again with an all too familiar ring to it. Her ex-husband's childhood had been difficult to say the least and his one attempt at counselling had ended in failure. He simply didn't think he had anything to discuss with the counsellor. His only attempt to reform was when Rachel had finally plucked up the courage to leave him and he'd attended one Alcoholic's Anonymous meeting. She had told him it was too little, too late and he had promptly blamed her for his non-attendance the following week. Apparently, he felt he could get better if it was for her, but he couldn't get better for himself.

"Our time is up now Sam. I'm not sure you got what you wanted out of our session, so I'm hesitant to recommend another one." Rachel didn't want to see this woman again. There were too many reminders of her own relationship with her ex-husband. It had been the loneliest place in the world being married to a man who preferred the company of a bottle of vodka than her and she felt desperately sorry for Sam's husband and for her step children.

Rachel counted herself as lucky. She no longer had to deal with the long, lonely nights when she took herself off to bed rather than watch the man she used to love drink himself into unconsciousness. Her escape had been traumatic, the violence had come in so many forms, she'd lost count. She really couldn't help this woman.

"Well, you've been helpful to a point. I don't need to come back because it's not me, it's the people around me who need therapy. You'd been very patient in listening to me Rachel, but I feel therapy is for those people who are much weaker than me. Thank you." Sam sounded sincere and appeared to truly believe her own rhetoric.

Keeping the incredulity out of her voice, Rachel wished Sam well and showed her as quickly as a heavily pregnant woman can move, out of the house and her life.

She returned to the safety of her kitchen. The Aga was pumping out it's incessant heat, keeping the cold feelings at bay. Rachel decided to make herself a herbal tea and lit a subtly fragranced candle, reassuring herself that this life she now had was well worth the actions of her murky past. It was particularly reassuring to think that her own children would hopefully avoid the machinations of a bitter step mother. It was unlikely their father would ever marry again or hold down any form of meaningful relationship.

Day Ten - The Children
23rd December

This was Rachel's last working day. The final client of the year was about to arrive and Rachel had six months of family time to look forward to. The client due to arrive this morning had been referred to her by the GP who was responsible for her. Rachel had some idea of her new client's history and it had sent shivers down her spine. She was considering the approach she would take when the doorbell rang.

For some reason, Rachel was slightly nervous as she waddled across the warm wooden boards of her hallway. As she opened the heavy front door she was greeted with the sight of a woman who was pale, tense and thin. This wasn't the type of healthy thinness displayed like a wealthy trophy by most women that Rachel saw, this was an ill-looking scrawniness that shouted trauma and stress.

The two ridiculously out-sized and under-sized women shook hands tentatively as Rachel asked her to follow her through the house.

"It's good to meet you Vicky. Please follow me into the garden, my office is at the end of the path so keep your shoes on."

As they walked, Vicky sniffed almost constantly. She held a damp tissue close to her nose, dabbing it from time to time as they entered the garden room.

"Please take a seat. Coffee? Tea? Water?" Enquired Rachel softly. Rachel was conscious that raising her voice above an audible whisper would be likely to damage this fragile woman even more.

"Coffee please." Rachel could barely hear Vicky's faint reply.

"Is a cappuccino ok? And do you take sugar?"

"That's fine. N-n-n-o I don't. Thank you." The tremor in Vicky's voice was more than apparent.

"Okay, let me get the drinks sorted and then we'll get started Vicky. Is that alright?" Rachel felt that checking in with Vicky was the right thing to do. She knew she'd been referred by her GP and on these occasions, it was never clear whether that was because the patient had asked for a referral or whether the Doctor had recommended it. Rachel knew Vicky had been on anti-depressants for three years now and understood the reasons she had been put on them. What she didn't know was how she was functioning day to day or if she was functioning at all.

Rachel still had misgivings as to whether her style of therapy was going to be enough for this poor woman, but felt that the referral had been made in good faith and wanted to see what she could do to help.

"Tell me why you're here Vicky, that might be a good place to start."

"I can't sleep, I have no appetite and I've not been able to work for three years. My doctor has tried me on different anti-depressants, but nothing seems to be working with me. I've failed to respond to treatment apparently." Her last words weren't bitter or resentful, she stated them with a very matter of fact tone which was consistent with everything she'd spoken so far.

"Did you have bereavement counselling Vicky?" Rachel steered clear of newly bereaved clients until they'd had some form of specialists counselling.

"Yes. For a whole year. I failed to respond to that too. I could barely talk for the first year after it happened. They thought I was mute because of the shock."

"It sounds like you reacted in a normal human way Vicky. Not all therapies work for everyone."

"I've failed." This was a statement, delivered with emphatic finality.

"You did your best Vicky. You did what you thought was best at the time with the resources you had available to you at the time. No one can know what another human being is capable of or might do. No one can mind read or predict the future." Whilst all of this was true, Rachel didn't think it would help Vicky. She still wasn't sure how to break through.

"Yes, the police said that when it happened. They said I'd done the right thing. What the hell do they know about doing the right thing. I suppose they wanted to make me feel better. You're a mother Rachel. You have a sixth sense about your kids don't you?"

"Yes, I do. Sometimes."

"You know when something isn't right and you also know when they're in danger. Don't you?" Vicky's questioning was making Rachel feel uncomfortable. She didn't like the direction it was taking. It made her feel exposed.

"Yes, Vicky, to a degree, but we still cannot predict what another human being may or may not do. We can't control the actions of another person and under no circumstances can we blame ourselves for the actions someone chooses to take." It was Rachel's turn to sound firm now. She wanted to steer Vicky away from blaming herself, it was about the only way she would be able to move on in her life.

"I know you're right Rachel. Rationally, I know you're right. If I'm logical about this, then of course you're right. It's not logical though is it? It's emotional and those feelings I have make me feel physically sick every single day of my miserable life. My throat closes when I try to eat and I can barely force soup down. When I close my eyes at night I run through all the scenarios that might have happened. All those moments in time when I could have done something to stop him. There are so many paths I could have taken and none of them would have led to where I am now." Tears started trickling down Vicky's pale, thin cheeks. Rachel motioned to the box of balm, infused super soft tissues next to the cappuccino which was now cold.

The idea of choosing a path forced a shiver down Rachel's spine. The baby inside her meant she was usually warm, too warm most of the time, but the thought of what 'might have been' was one of the many scenarios Rachel had played out over the years. She still did. There was one path she preferred not to acknowledge in her own life.

She'd shut the door, bolted it and thrown away the key which led down that particular route.

"Okay Vicky, I'm getting an understanding of how you're stuck. There's a type of therapy called time line which might help you let go of the guilt you feel. I've used it many times before with lots of different clients and it always gets a good result for them. Are you happy to give it a go?"

"Anything is worth trying Rachel. I know I can't go on like this. My body is almost as broken as my mind. How does it work?"

"It's works differently with different people Vicky, I know how it worked for me because I know how I processed it in my head, but I'm not sure how it will work for you. The only way you'll know is if you try it."

"Okay. Let's give it go." Vicky's response gave an inkling of a slightly lighter frame of mind. At least curiosity was taking her mind off her current state of existence.

Rachel ran through the process slowly. She asked Vicky to imagine herself floating above herself in the garden room and looking down on herself in the chair. Vicky closed her eyes and looked peaceful as she followed Rachel's carefully worded instructions.

"Now float gently higher, higher into the sky Vicky, right up to the edge of space. Remember the guy who went to the edge of space on his jet pack. The Red Bull guy."

Vicky nodded and smiled. It was the first time Rachel had seen her smile and it lifted her entire body as well as her face. She had been carefree and pretty once.

"Go all the way up to the edge of space and look down on yourself sitting in the chair in my garden room. You'll be a tiny dot. Can you see yourself Vicky?" Rachel liked to check her clients were following her instructions to the letter. Her client nodded.

"Okay, now look back over your past and notice the first event where you felt this guilt." Vicky's features tightened as she imagined going back in time. Rachel tapped the glass of water next to her and told Vicky she was safely concealed in a glass ball high above the events with a solid glass floor beneath her, keeping her secure.

Rachel patiently took Vicky through the next few steps of the process and as she did so, her body started to shake uncontrollably.

"It's okay Vicky. It's okay. You're safe in your glass ball above the glass floor, high up in the sky, nothing's getting through. You're safe Vicky." Rachel had learned through years of experience that her clients got through this exercise better if she continued to reassure them of their safety and tap the glass so their brains would be fooled into thinking they really were in a glass ball, above a glass floor.

Vicky breathed heavily.

"Let's go back way before the first event that caused the guilt. Let me know when you're there."

Vicky nodded and Rachel continued.

"How do you feel?"

"Free." Vicky's voice was relaxed and almost sounded content. A hint of a smile appeared at the corner of her mouth, then abruptly vanished.

"He wasn't in my life then. I was free. It was bliss." Rachel didn't want Vicky to start blaming herself again, so she quickly moved on.

"Okay, so what do you know now that will be useful to take with you into the future and enable you to let go of the guilt. Whatever that learning is, - you can keep hold of it for the future."

"I didn't know. I didn't know." Her words were fervent. The relief was palpable.

"Can you turn that into a positive feeling that's going to be useful to you in the future Vicky?" Rachel wanted Vicky to focus on the things she could do, rather than the things she couldn't.

"I can only do what I think is right at the time I do it."

"When you say that Vicky, how does it feel?"

"Calm. I feel calm." Her voice sounded calm and her face softened to reveal a woman more comfortable in her own skin.

"Hold that feeling of calm in your body Vicky and make it bigger. Give it a colour or shape if you want to and imagine it filling you from the top of your head right down to the soles of your feet. Take it with you as you travel high up above your past towards the first event that caused you to feel guilt." Rachel could see that Vicky was responding well and carried on with the timeline process.

As Vicky went deep into the event which was the root cause of her emotional dis-ease and very rapidly came out of it again, guided carefully by Rachel, she applied her calm feeling and the tears of relief began to flow freely.

Rachel finished the session by asking Vicky to look out into her future and apply her calmness to her future, making sure there'd be no need to feel the pressure of guilt she had been feeling when she came to the door.

Vicky sobbed heavily. "What did you do? I can't believe how different I feel. That dead weight I've been carrying around for three years has gone. It's sounds strange Rachel, but I finally feel ready to grieve for my children. I can stop blaming myself for what that bastard did and start remembering my beautiful children the way I want to remember them. You know I haven't been able to visit their graves? I didn't feel I deserved to honour them."

"You loved your children Vicky. You loved them so much, you followed all the rules. You did exactly what the law said you should do and you did that because you loved them." Rachel recalled her own encounter with the Sheriff Court, remembering how badly the system had let her down.

Rosie and Sam had been young when Rachel left her ex-husband. Rosie was in the early years of primary school and Ben had just joined a pre-school nursery. Her estranged husband had received a huge lump sum from the sale of the ex-marital home and he'd been able to buy himself a flat in town as well as a small cottage in the country. Rachel found herself living in a tiny three-bedroomed flat in the city, but with the relative security of her own business which gave her a decent income.

Each time the kids came back home from the cottage with their dad, they'd tell her tales of pet kittens and rabbits being purchased, bulbs being planted in the garden and the promise of a tree-house in the garden. None of these things sounded like temporary matters suited to the odd weekend in the cottage, which is how her ex had described his second home. Rachel began to feel very uneasy about his intentions and suspected he wanted to move the children in with him. She was terrified he would drink himself into a stupor and leave a candle burning or something equally as forgetful. Her greatest nightmare was that of her children inhaling toxic smoke in their beds at night whilst their father lay in a vodka induced state of unconsciousness.

When he proposed having the kids with him in the cottage, thirty miles from their school during the time he had them in the week, Rachel had despaired. The kids would have to get up at 6am two days a week and take the notoriously dangerous country road from the cottage, over the hills, through the commuter traffic to school. On top of these risks, Rachel also knew he was likely to be over the alcohol limit and unfit to drive. Her greatest fears were being realised and she acted in the only way she knew how. She did the right thing and went through her solicitor to gain a temporary ban on him taking the kids outside of the city boundaries.

The court hearing followed and in an absolute act of cowardice and incompetence the Sheriff decided not to make a decision, declaring that he thought the parents had been able to make mutually agreeable decisions to date and that they could make a decision about this matter between themselves without his intervention.

Rachel had almost vomited with shock and her lawyer was angry that the Sheriff who was paid to make decisions, had singularly failed in his role. She wanted to scream and shout about the truth; the drinking, the verbal abuse, the control, the threats and so much more, but doing the right thing meant she couldn't do that. She had to follow the process, stick to the law and allow her children to spend time with a man who she knew was a danger to their safety. She had no way of proving it though. She didn't have any marks on her body. There was no evidence. No witnesses. People thought she was the career bitch who had ditched her dutiful house husband for a better offer.

The truth was she alone. No one believed her. Not even her own mother.

"Vicky. Nothing, I can say will ever bring your children back. The system let you and your children down badly. They trusted the word of a respectable firearms police officer and gave his opinion more weight than yours Vicky. Your warnings weren't listened to and dismissed as vindictive or hysterical."

The news reports at the time had described how Vicky's estranged husband had held a shotgun license and had had it renewed only two months before he shot his own children and then turned the gun on himself. Questions had been asked regarding the decision made by the local firearms officer, but no action had been taken. At the time, the husband appeared mentally stable. It was only his estranged wife who had caused a fuss. The news reports portrayed her as an unhinged hysterical ex-wife with a grudge to bear. Pictures had been published of her looking wide eyed with tears, whilst the father was pictured in his smart suit, holding hands with his two children as they looked at him adoringly.

He had the sensible job with the accountancy firm, whilst she was the stay at home mum. Journalists had made Vicky out to be a lazy woman with nothing to do all day except go to the gym whilst her hard working husband funded her ladies who lunch lifestyle. The kids were already at school, so Vicky did have free time. What she also had was an insight into the control her husband exerted over all their lives. Not one reporter had been interested to know about the lack of access she had to the family finances or the way her husband checked the mileage on her car to make sure she hadn't driven anywhere beyond the school, the gym or the supermarket.

It's easy to judge when you don't know the full story. The headlines only give you what they want you to believe. Just enough information to steer you in the direction they want to you to go in.

Rachel was now witnessing the other side of the story. The side the papers didn't want you to see or hear.

Vicky was sobbing quietly as Rachel spoke to her. Every fibre of her being was grieving, each cell was aching with pain as she sat crumpled, deflated and lost in the chair.

"I'm so sorry I did the right thing Rachel. If I'd have killed him like I wanted to, I might have served a lengthy prison sentence, but my darling children might still be alive."

"I know Vicky, but you can't think like that. So many things might or might not have happened. You're here now and you're free to honour their memory. What would you like to do to begin healing yourself?"

"What would you have done Rachel, if you'd have been in my shoes?" The question came out of the blue and put Rachel on the back foot. She paused, buying some time before she answered.

"Well, I-I-I'm not sure." She stuttered, feeling the discomfort rise in her body. She hoped she wasn't going red.

"I'm sorry Rachel, that was an unfair question. No one knows how they'll act until they're in that situation. Right?"

Rachel hoped that her visible sigh of relief had gone undetected. She quickly returned to the subject of Vicky's future as a way to finish the session and to return to the safety of her kitchen.

"Okay, for next time, I'd like you to have thought about the legacy you want to create in memory of your children. It can be anything, no matter how seemingly small. It will be important to you."

"Thanks Rachel, I will. For the first time in years, I feel able to think about the future, even in a small way." Rachel witnessed Vicky's smile for the first time and felt she'd done some good work. She'd find a way to see Vicky whilst she was on maternity leave and support her in any way she could.

As Rachel waved goodbye to Vicky, the phrase, 'there but for the grace of god go I,' ran through her head. She'd made sure her children were safe. For good.

Day Eleven - The Father
24th December

"Mum!" The early morning wake up call from Sam jolted Rachel out of her deep slumber. She'd had a good night's sleep for a change, managing to adjust the numerous pillows around her over-stretched body in just the right way. She hadn't even had to get up to go to the toilet.

It was Christmas Eve, the kids were now off school and they were excited about the presents they imagined they were about to receive.

Sam stood next to her, waiting expectantly for a reply.

"Yes Sam. What is it?" mumbled Rachel, unable to open her eyes. She felt Eddie shift his position next to her, determined to remain asleep.

"Is dad coming to pick us up this year? It's his turn isn't it?"

Rachel knew she would have to get up to talk about this. It wasn't a conversation she could have from her pillow.

"I'm getting up now Sam. I'll get you some breakfast and we'll have a chat. Go and put the television on and I'll be down in a minute."

Rachel heaved herself out of bed and lumbered into the bathroom, catching a glimpse of her bulk in the mirror and wondering how the hell her body had managed to morph itself into this state for the third time in her life.

There was an age gap of eight years between Sam and the new baby and Rachel's body wasn't as supple or pliable as it had been in her late twenties. She was two years away from being forty and her body had coped with the pregnancy, but hadn't particularly welcomed it. She wondered how women in their forties got on and shuddered at the thought of giving birth whilst contending with the aches and pains which were the inevitable outcomes of a well-used body.

She had been pretty fit when she conceived, but in her usual manner, had stuffed her face full of well buttered toasted bagels topped with expensive French blueberry preserve. It was her morning treat after dropping the kids off at school. She'd been so hungry during this pregnancy that she'd had to get up in the night on a few occasions to stuff a bowl full of Special K in her mouth. When she's heard a mum health guru on Woman's Hour claim that women only needed a few extra calories during pregnancy which amounted to a single slice of wholemeal toast with butter, Rachel had almost spat her jam coated bagel out. This same mum guru had claimed to get straight back into her skinny jeans after giving birth. Rachel's response had been to shout, "fuck off," very loudly at the radio. There were limits to her sisterhood morals.

She sat heavily on the toilet to pee and attempted to work out how she was going to explain to Sam and his sister Rosie that they wouldn't be seeing their dad at Christmas, or anytime soon. They'd not seen him for a year and had asked about him on the odd occasion, but had been content to be told that he was travelling abroad.

Their father had always been unreliable. He rarely contacted his two children unprompted and only took them when he felt like it. His interest in his children had waned as he realised he couldn't get his hands on the Child Benefit or win more money from Rachel through the courts if he looked after them. His application to receive half the Child Benefit had been one of his many tactics to gain more money from Rachel. It had failed because his attempts to look after them for fifty percent of the time had dwindled to seeing them once a week on a Saturday night.

Whenever an arrangement had been organised, he always managed to find a way to change it. He found numerous excuses to reduce his time with his children and he usually blamed Rachel. In his eyes, she'd difficult or uncompromising when he asked for changes. In reality, she gladly accepted any additional time with her kids and simply accommodated his demands, relieved that they were spending less and less time with a man who she knew would be drinking heavily whilst in charge of her kids.

Since the incident with the remote cottage, Rachel had been very wary of allowing the children to travel abroad with their father. He'd taken them away the previous summer to Spain with his sensible girlfriend. Rachel was genuinely happy that she was travelling with the children because she knew she could trust her. Suki was a beautiful soul with a very kind heart. Rachel had attempted to befriend her and get to know her, but she was clearly suspicious of Rachel's motives. She guessed her ex-husband had been poisoning her mind against her and knew that he was very good at getting people to believe what he wanted them to believe.

Suki was therefore polite towards Rachel, but not warm. Happily, her children loved her and talked very fondly about her which is why Rachel was reassured by her presence on their trip abroad. Rosie had even mentioned that Suki meditated and believed in Buddhism and for a very brief period Rosie had attempted meditation herself. Rachel had viewed this as endearing and felt that meditating was probably more positive for Rosie than focusing on her unreliable father and his erratic behaviour.

This hadn't stopped Rachel fretting throughout their time away though. She had been extremely reluctant to give him their passports, but had no choice. On the text messages between each other on their return, Rachel had repeatedly asked for the passports to be included in their bags when she picked them up. She'd emptied their bags, searching frantically for the small burgundy coloured documents without success. She'd texted him to find out where they were and received one of his usual cryptic replies: "I've got them" and "you won't be needing them anymore."

This had sent a shiver down Rachel's spine. She had tried not to panic, but felt the heat rising from her knotting stomach up through her throat to the point where swallowing had become difficult. This had been one of the multitude of occasions where she'd had to hide her true feelings from the kids. She had to pretend that everything was ok.

Keep being normal. Pretend nothing is wrong. Those had been her mantras throughout her marriage and now they continued as she extricated herself from this man.

Despite her gentle requests, the passports didn't appear. It was the last element of control he had and he wasn't going to let go of it easily. Rachel recalled her gut-wrenching stress throughout the year, unable to extricate the all-important passports from her unstable husband. Additional threats had emerged over the months leading up to Christmas last year. He dropped hints about selling his flat, leaving for a warmer climate and casually mentioned the benefits of receiving an overseas education for kids. Rachel couldn't retaliate as he always made sure Rosie and Sam were in earshot. She felt increasingly sick at the thought of seeing him and knew he was planning to do something. She just didn't know what it would be.

Her judgement was clouded by the deep distrust of the legal system. She'd already been badly let down by it and couldn't fully trust that a father in possession of his kid's passports would be prevented from leaving the country permanently. Her imagination projected a nightmare scenario of long court battles, police searches across Europe and two terrified children missing their mum. No, he couldn't be allowed to carry out his threats. She had to stop him.

As she washed her hands, Rachel decided that honesty was the best policy with Sam and Rosie. She took a deep breath and carefully descended the stairs, entering the living room with a fixed smile and a cheery voice,

"Kids." Rosie had joined her brother on the sofa and they were busy staring blankly at "Dick and Dom in the Bungalow", a favourite of theirs.

"Yeah." They weren't really paying attention so Rachel switched the TV off. Now she had their full attention.

"Mum!" They exclaimed in unison.

"It's about your dad."

"Is he coming to pick us up?" Enquired Sam hopefully. Rosie was silent and sullen. She'd been very angry when Rachel had left their father. Being old enough to realise what divorce meant, but still too young to understand the implications of alcoholism or abuse, Rachel had simply asked her daughter to trust her decision to leave their father.

She'd explained carefully that he was not a good person for her mum to live with and that she'd left because she wanted to protect Rosie and Sam from arguments and upset that had been increasingly part of the family routine.

"You're going to have to trust me Rosie. When you're old enough, I'll be able to explain it to you better. All you need to know right now is that I've left him because I love you and Sam so much and it's the best way I know how to protect you." Rachel had looked deep into Rosie's eyes, hoping that her young mind would grasp what she was being told.

Children have to accept the version of the truth that their parents tell them. They have no choice. Everything they've ever learned and trust comes from their parents and so Rosie had no choice but to accept what her mum was telling her. Whether she thought it was true or not was another matter.

Rosie's sullen expression gave Rachel cause for concern, but she ploughed on, hoping her lies would sound convincing.

"Your dad hasn't been in touch since last Christmas and as you know I think he's gone abroad."

Rosie and Sam looked at their mother with blank faces. She thought she detected a slight frown on Sam's forehead, but Rosie's face was unreadable.

"Sorry kids."

"It's alright mum. Can you put the TV back on, it's Dick and Dom."

"Sure. Are you ok with this?"

"Yeah. We've not seen him for ages." Said Rosie. "And to be honest, he was always pretty unreliable anyway. I think he's moved to France or Spain with Suki."

"I think you're probably right Rosie. It's just like your dad to move abroad and not tell anyone."

"He'll phone us when he remembers." Said Sam hopefully.

"Maybe." Rachel responded without conviction, something Rosie picked up on immediately.

"Do you think we'll ever see him again?" She asked
"I'm not sure Rosie. If I know your dad, I doubt it. He was seeing less and less of you anyway wasn't he? He didn't send you birthday cards this year either."

"Yeah. I guess Eddie is our dad now." This was the first time Rosie had made the connection between Eddie who was one hundred percent reliable and always there for this kids and his role as her father.

"I guess he is Rosie."

"That's alright mum, I like Eddie." Sam's enthusiasm for Eddie was obvious, they were inseparable most of the time. He'd taken Eddie to football, karate and cub camp, which Sam loved. It was one of Rachel's criteria for any man who entered into her life after she left their father. He must get on with her kids, it had been a deal breaker with a couple of hopeful contenders. Eddie had been different from the start. He'd made sure the kids were included in all kinds of activities and he made them both laugh, something that had always been lacking with their biological father.

"Are you two ok for breakfast?" Rachel felt the time was right to move the conversation on. After all, how do you explain to your kids that they're never going to see their dad again?

"We're fine thanks mum. We'll get some Rice Krispies once this has finished." Rosie spoke for her and Sam as she often did.

"Right. I'll leave you to it. I'll be upstairs getting dressed if you need me."

Rachel heaved her bulk back up the stairs. She returned to bed, propping herself up with her pillow collection. Eddie was snoring gently, pretending to be in a deep sleep.

"I've told the kids they're unlikely to see their father ever again." Rachel knew he would be able to hear.

"Oh." Came the muffled reply from under the duvet.

"Rosie said she thought you could be her dad now."

"That's nice." Eddie's voice was non-committal. He very rarely made a drama out of anything, which was one of the qualities Rachel loved about him. It was also one of qualities that frustrated her the most. She wanted a reaction from him on this occasion. A romantic, 'that's wonderful darling, we can now call ourselves a proper family' or something along those lines. That's what would have happened in a romantic novel: the handsome lover would have scooped his fecund wife up into his arms and told her it was all going to be alright now because he was their father and their protector.

Life didn't play out like the romantic novels suggested they would. The perfect life with its minor trials and tribulations inserted into the story for dramatic effect didn't always end happily the way we like them to. Sometimes, the prince turns out to be a toad and the heroine isn't the woman we think she is or ought to be.

Whilst Rachel's imagination was wandering off into Bronte territory, she felt a sudden paid across her swollen stomach. She immediately recognised it as a contraction. She ignored it and as she did so she slowly became aware of a dull ache in her lower back. She also knew what this meant. The baby was on its way. A little early perhaps, but nothing that would cause concern.

She shifted uncomfortably against the pillows. Then another sharp contraction shot across her belly.

"Eddie." She nudged him gently with her elbow.

"Hmmm?" He mumbled.

"I think the baby's coming today."

He turned his head sharply towards Rachel and looked up at her.

"You're joking." His voice was slightly incredulous.

"No. I've had a couple of contractions in quick succession and I've got a dull ache in my lower back. I know the signs." Rachel was very matter of fact. Her body knew what was coming and she'd had two straight forward births so the next few hours held no fear for her.

"I'll have a bath to ease the pain."

"Are you sure?" There was the tiniest hint of panic in Eddie's voice. He'd not been through this before and had no idea what was coming.

"Yeah. It's fine. It really helps to relax your body in preparation for the birth."

"I'll run it for you then." Rachel found his offer sweet, but wanted to be active to take her mind off the increasing levels of discomfort.

"It's ok sweetheart, I want to keep moving. You get the kids ready to go to my brother's, I think we'll be busy for the rest of the day."

Rachel absentmindedly prepared her bath, as she eased herself into it she compared her current situation to the one she had been in only a year earlier. Her pregnancy had been a welcome distraction to the confused feelings she'd been having in the first few months of the year.

She'd attempted to block out the images of last Christmas Eve, most of the time achieving a neutral state of mind rather than the inner peace she craved. On occasions, her moods had been quite black and she had felt herself slipping into a chasm of guilt and self-loathing. It was only her training as a therapist that had been her saving grace.

The kids had been spending some rare time with their father just before Christmas last year and Rachel had gone to pick them up a few days before Christmas Eve as they had agreed. She'd been very wary of his motives and had questioned him closely about where he intended to take them. He was his usual vague self and then she'd received a text which had turned her blood to ice. "I've still got their passports. It's nearly time."

Rachel felt another surge across her stretched stomach, the baby was definitely on its way. This child had a father who would never torture Rachel like her ex had done over the years. His last text had been the final straw for Rachel. She'd reached the end of her tether. She was determined that she would put an end to his manipulation and his control. For months he'd behaved reasonably, lulled her into a false sense of security and yet he'd continued with the veiled threats. His words didn't match his behaviour, something Rachel found incredibly confusing. She'd convinced herself that he had finally accepted her new relationship with Eddie and was content that she was the primary career for the children. He'd seen so little of Rosie and Sam that she had hoped he'd moved on in his life and would leave them all alone. Her firm belief in the goodness of human beings was the thread she'd been clinging onto. He couldn't take his kids overseas, could he? Would he actually go through with it?

His text made her realise with a stab of panic that this could happen. He would never be content to see her happy and free. He would always find a way to control her, to make her feel insecure and to threaten her peace of mind. She'd spent years feeling uncertain. Years, looking over her shoulder, choosing her words carefully and painstakingly adjusting her tone of voice so he wouldn't react. Nothing she did made a difference. He would seem calm and reasonable one minute and the next he would be shouting at her, calling her a whore and an unfit mother and threatening to fight for control over the kid's lives.

He'd told her she couldn't watch Sam in his swimming gala because he wanted to go. Rachel had promised to sit on the other side of the huge viewing area by the pool and yet this had not been enough to satisfy his need for control.

"If you go, I won't let Sam take part." Had been his response.

Rachel had begged and pleaded with him. This was Sam's first swimming gala and she was desperate to watch her son.

"But you came to the kid's Christmas concert and I was there too." Was Rachel reasoned response.

"I've decided you can't come to his gala because I don't want to be in the same building as you." Rachel knew his argument was irrational and unreasonable, but she had no choice. She'd missed Sam's gala and later found out that his father hadn't taken him in the end anyway. Sam had been devastated. He'd cried himself to sleep and announced the following day that he was going to give up his swimming lessons. When Rachel had tried to talk to his father about it, he'd blamed Sam's distress on her desire to turn his son against him. He'd told her flatly that it was her fault Sam didn't want to have swimming lessons.

It broke her heart because she knew how much her son had been looking forward to the gala. How many more times was she going to allow this man to dictate the way she and her children lived their lives. She knew for certain that he had to be stopped.

The bath water was getting cold and her contractions were increasing in intensity. It was time to get out, put some comfortable clothes on and prepare for a trip to the hospital.

Rachel carefully dried herself and placed the sticky pads of the TENS machine onto her back, either side of her spine. She had no idea whether the machine actually worked or whether it was a happy distraction, either way, she'd used it for her first two labours and was confident it would see her through the third.

The doorbell rang. Rachel caught her breath. She'd been expecting a call for months now so each and every time the bell rang unexpectedly, she anticipated the worse. She peered out of the bedroom window and saw her brother's car parked on the street. She breathed heavily, realising her worst fears had not yet been realised.

After all, Rachel had been very careful. She'd paid cash for the seemingly innocuous vodka and made sure her hood was up as she entered and exited the off license. It was a cold December day and wearing a hood, gloves and scarf looked perfectly normal. She made sure she bought cranberry juice to go with the vodka and used her unmarked bag for life to carry her purchases to her ex-husband's flat.

She knew he'd been taking Antabuse tablets for several weeks. It was the only way he'd managed to convince Rachel that he was capable of looking after Sam and Rosie for a few days. Suki had confirmed it and put Rachel's mind at ease. He'd taken the tablets whilst she they were married during one of his many attempts to give up alcohol. He always managed to stop taking them just before a birthday or a celebration so he could drink.

He'd been violently sick one New Year's Eve early on in their relationship when he hadn't given enough time for the Antabuse tablets time to leave his system. On that occasion Rachel had carefully placed him in the recovery position and left him to it. This time she had no intention of being there to help him.

Feeling very much in control, Rachel had carefully placed the vodka on the work surface in his kitchen whilst he was gathering the kid's stuff together. It was a large bottle. Large enough to make him dead drunk.

She'd checked he was still taking the tablets before leaving as calmly as possible from his flat with her precious charges. He'd been satisfactorily smug in his response, acting surprised that she had to ask. She remembered his last words to her,

"Here are the passports." He waved them in front of her face, taunting her with the tiny amount of power he had left.

"If I want to take the kids abroad to live with me, I will and there is nothing you can do to stop me. You'll never know when I choose to do it, we'll be gone. I'd love to see your smug face then Rachel."

"Alistair, be reasonable. Rosie and Sam have their lives here. They're happy and settled. We've just about managed to divorce without causing too much damage to them. Please give me their passports." She rarely used his name. It wasn't a word she cared to repeat very often, but on this occasion, she needed to appeal to the more humane side of his personality.

He laughed at her and walked away, calling the kids as he did so, leaving Rachel with no choice but to concede. She wasn't prepared to fight with him in front of the children. She was forced to control her powerful emotions, the pure hatred that welled up inside of her drove her to conclude that the action she was about to take was fully justified.

She was pleased she'd found his Antabuse tablets in the kitchen cupboard as she opened them up, her hands shook with anger. She selected two capsules from the blister pack, opened them up and carefully emptied the powdery contents into the bottle of vodka. His Christmas present was ready for him to consume whenever he felt like it. She wanted to be as sure as she possible that his night would be a short one. She'd been careful to keep her gloves on as she screwed the cap back on as tightly as she could. He would never notice that the bottle had already been opened. She knew him well enough to know that the desire to drink would be overwhelming for him, so long as he could get into the bottle, he would't care. She gave it a shake to disperse the powder and left it on the work surface in his kitchen. He would do the rest for her.

Rachel got the kid's bags together and told them to give their dad a hug. The three of them walked out of his flat, leaving him to the fate he decided to choose for himself. Rachel hoped it was the last time he would be able to frighten her ever again.

Day Twelve – Christmas Dinner

December 25th

Rachel arrived home around 10am on Christmas morning. Eddie helped her out of the car and then leaned into the back seat to release the seatbelt which was holding the Stage One car seat firmly in place. Nestled into the seat was a tiny new life: Scarlett had appeared late afternoon on Christmas Eve and was perfect in every way. Her crop of downy blonde hair and sharp blue eyes reflected back into her proud father's face as he carried her gently to the front door of their home.

There was no doubt who's child she was. She was the spitting image of Eddie, the midwives had told him as they passed her to him in a bundle of blankets immediately after the chord was cut. He held her momentarily and instantly fell in love with his new daughter. The midwife then gently lifted her away from her doting father and handed her to Rachel who lay propped up in bed, exhausted but overjoyed at the birth of her third child, her second daughter. Scarlett nuzzled her breast and began latching on as only new borns can do. To everyone's great relief, she fed quickly and easily. Rachel recognised that familiar feeling of another human life, suckling at her breast, nurturing the child she had already carried and fed for nine months.

The small group were left in peace as the midwives tidied up around them. There was a silence in labour wards that people find hard to understand. Films and TV make us think that they're noisy, frantic wards, but in fact, they're calm, quiet places where mother's and father's stare transfixed into the faces of their newly born offspring. Each one, a tiny miracle of nature. Each one with its own destiny ahead of it. Each new life born with hope, love and good intentions. Where they end up is entirely in the hands of the adults who care for them. Whether they're loved, neglected, abused or cherished is within the gift of the people who care for them. The start every baby gets in life begins with the conception and something that started as a lottery, continues well into early adulthood when the person finally gets to make their own choices.

Those choices are of course largely dictated by their environment and their genes, until we learn otherwise.

Eddie had gone outside to work his way through the list of phone calls, telling everyone the good news, both mum and baby were in good form and should be home in time for Christmas dinner.

Rosie and Sam were at the front door eagerly awaiting the arrival of their new sister. Their uncle, Rachel's brother was there too. He didn't have kids of his own, preferring the bachelor lifestyle of international travel with work and a smart penthouse apartment in the centre of town. He was a good uncle though and spoilt his niece and nephew rotten. He now had a new niece to spoil and it began with a small Steiff rabbit with a red pinafore and fluffy white tail. He handed the gift to Scarlett who stared wide-eyed at her new surroundings as she was carefully lifted into Rosie's waiting arms.

This was the happiest Rachel had ever been. Her family was complete. They were all content, all healthy and most importantly all together. Nothing could drive them apart now. No court in the land could possibly rule that Sam and Rosie's father had the right to take them abroad now. Even with the gloomy prospect that he might still be living close by, Rachel was certain that he would leave them alone. She dare not contemplate the consequences of her actions a year ago. She had told herself so many times that he might not have drunk the vodka, he might not have been sick and he might not have choked on his own vomit. He might have been found by his girlfriend Suki just in time to be resuscitated and they might be living happily ever after in Spain, just as he had threatened to do, except the children were with her now, safe and sound.

She couldn't think about that now. The day was too special to allow him to enter her thoughts. Eddie made sure she was comfortable on the family sofa in the living room and ushered the older children into the kitchen to help their uncle get the Christmas Dinner started. Scarlett lay contented in her Moses basket with her new rabbit placed next to her. She would never experience the trauma of living with an alcoholic parent. Eddie hardly ever drank. She would only know love, kindness and togetherness. Her father would protect her, nurture her, fill her with confidence and be there for her when she needed him. He would never let her down.

Rachel drifted off to sleep whilst the household prepared Christmas. As she did so, she attempted to recall the last Christmas she'd had with the kids before she left their father. The image of the memory was no longer there. She searched for the pictures in her head and couldn't find them anywhere. This brought her back out of her dreamy state and she opened her eyes. She tried to recall Sam's second birthday and couldn't conjure that up either or Rosie's fifth birthday. Where were these important memories? Then she realised she barely recollected the last two years of her life with her ex husband. She got occasional glimpses of a chair being thrown or a stream of angry abuse about her lack of suitability as a mother and a wife. She shuddered at the thought of one his last threats to take what he wanted from her whenever he wanted it. Whilst he had never raped her, the threat he had made was clear: he could and would if he wanted to.

Rachel picked Scarlett up and held her to her heart. She lay back down with her new baby resting softly across her chest. She was safe now. Nothing was going to threaten her physically or emotionally anymore. Those days were long gone. She would make new memories with her new family. She would savour every single moment and commit every holiday and special occasion to her memory banks. Rachel knew family life wouldn't be a constant round of Cath Kidston cookie cutter meals or holidays, she knew it would include the full range of messy emotions, arguments and unhappy times too. That was the point though: it would be normal. No one would be treading on egg shells wondering what mood Eddie was in. Rosie wouldn't have to pretend to be the perfect girl in order to avoid the ascorbic comments of her father. Latterly, he'd commented on how fat her bottom was getting and had told her she'd better lose weight. When Rachel had tackled him about his comments after a tearful conversation with Rosie he called her a liar and told her she'd been putting ideas into his daughter's head in order to turn her against him.

Scarlett woke Rachel up with a soft mewling sound. It meant she was hungry. The pair quickly settled into a comfortable position and Scarlett took her fill from Rachel. Mother looked down at daughter with a deep love in her eyes. The bond had been firmly formed and would never be broken. How quickly a mother develops the bond which means she would lay down her life for her children is incredible. For Rachel, it was almost instantaneous at the birth of each of her children. The feeling was overwhelming at times as well as deeply fulfilling. She could never be cruel to her children, she could never hit them or call them vile names like her own mother had done to her. Her bond was too great for her to be physically able to inflict that kind of pain on her kids. Scarlett was no different. She loved all three of them equally.

Eddie walked into the peaceful scene and announced Christmas dinner was ready.

"Prefect timing. Our daughter had just finished her Christmas dinner too."

Eddie smiled and scooped his daughter up into his arms, admiring her with an air of wonderment before placing her carefully back into her Moses Basket. He carried her through to the kitchen dining area where the table had been beautifully laid with Christmas candles, napkins and a holly centre peace which Rosie had been carefully preparing for the occasion.

Sam held his mum's hand and showed her to her seat at the head of the table.

"You sit here mum. This is your special place now." He beamed proudly at her and helped her into the chair.

"Thank you son." Rachel held back a tear, feeling the full significance of the moment. She looked around the table at her family and saw them all busily helping themselves to the piles of carrots and mountains of crisp golden brown roast potatoes. The turkey sat in pride of place in the middle of the table surrounded by pigs in blankets and neat little balls of sage and onion stuffing. Her brother had done them all proud, it was a true feast for the eyes.

"Shall I carve?" Eddie asked.

"I think you should, it's not often you get to carve a turkey on Christmas Day surrounded by your family and new baby daughter." Rachel responded

"You don't mind do you Chris?" She addressed the question to her brother just in case he was offended.

"No, go ahead. I've done my bit now. I can return to being my usual selfish self with no responsibilities." He knocked back a large glass of red wine as he surveyed the scene and smiled contentedly to himself.

"Are you hungry kids?" Eddie asked, knowingly.

"Starving!" They replied in unison.

A reverential hush descended as Eddie carefully carved the succulent bird. Everyone's mouth was watering and their eyes were fixed on the meat falling away from the carcass. Once everyone had their plates piled high with veg, potatoes, meat and covered in rich gravy, the chatter started up again. This time it was with warm comments about the deliciousness of the food, the moistness of the meat and the perfection of the crispy roast potatoes.

"Cheers everyone!" Eddie raised his glass.

"Here's to many more happy Christmas's to come."

"Here, here!" Came the reply from the room.

As sips of wine and cola were taken by the adults and the kids respectively. The doorbell rang.

Rachel's body immediately tensed up. She knew what this would be about. A feeling deep in her gut told her that this was not going to be someone making a social call.

"I wonder who that could be?" Eddie asked without expecting a reply.

He stood up and walked through the hallway to the front door.

Rachel stopped eating and looked across at her children. They were oblivious to her change in mood and were hungrily stuffing their faces full of Christmas dinner.

She strained to hear the voices from the front of the house. She looked across at her brother who had also stopped eating and was attempting to hear what was going on.

A pale faced Eddie walked back into the room followed by two police officers. One female and one male. Rachel's stomach twisted painfully and her mouth went bone dry.

"Rachel Jenkins?" The police woman's voice was matter of fact.

"Yes." Rachel desperately tried to keep the terror she was feeling inside from voice.

"Can we have a word with you? In private."

Everyone in the room looked at Rachel.

"Yes. Yes, of course." She got up and put her napkin on the table, leaving her unfinished Christmas dinner behind.

"Follow me, we'll sit in the living room whilst the others finish their dinner." As Rachel left the room she smiled weakly at Eddie. "Please, carry on eating without me."

As she took the half a dozen footsteps from the kitchen dining area through the hallway and into the living room, Rachel's mind was sprinting through the myriad of possible scenarios. Had they come to arrest her? Would they be taking her away? She hadn't had time to express any milk yet and Scarlett would be due another feed in an hour or so. It felt like an age before they were all seated in the living room, a place where only half an hour previously she had finally found peace with the world.

The police officers perched on the edge of the sofa and showed no emotion. Rachel couldn't read anything from their expressions, something she found frustrating because she was normally so good at reading people.

"Do you know an Alasdair McEwan?"

"Yes, he's my ex-husband. Why?" Rachel did not believe in a god, she was firmly in the atheist camp and yet she found herself pleading to god, any god that would listen for this to be not happening. Not today. Not today of all days.

"We've found a body which we believe to be Mr McEwan and we have reason to believe you were the last person to see him alive."

Rachel's world began to collapse around her. She saw the carefully managed framework of her life slowly melting away into nothing. She shivered and felt terribly, terribly cold and very alone.

"Oh." Rachel didn't know what to say. There were no words to describe the feelings she was experiencing at that moment in time.

"When did you last see Mr McEwan, Mrs Jenkins?" Still no expression, still no clue as to what these people were thinking.

"Last year. A few days before Christmas Eve. I picked the kids up from him as it was my turn to have them for Christmas." She didn't want to tell them too much, but she wanted to make sure she sounded helpful.

"And you haven't seen or heard from him since?" The policewoman sounded almost sarcastic.

"No. Nothing." Rachel replied honestly.

"You didn't think that was strange considering he's the father of your two eldest children?" again, Rachel thought she heard a hint of sarcasm in this woman's tone of voice. She controlled the tone of her response to avoid rising to the bait.

"No. He's been pretty unreliable over the years and I often didn't hear from him for weeks or even months at a time. I assumed he'd moved to Spain with Suki."

"We contacted Suki yesterday and she hadn't seen him since just before last Christmas either. She assumed he'd disappeared to Spain after they split up." The policeman took the role of good cop and his voice was kinder than his colleague's.

"They split up?"

"Yes, we thought you were aware of that." Came the matter of fact response.

"No. I thought they were very much a couple and had decided to start a new life together abroad." Rachel wondered whether she had mentioned her theory about Spain once too many times. The thought crossed her mind that this made her sound guilty. She made a mental note not to mention it again.

She wasn't surprised Suki and Alasdair had split up. She knew only too well how difficult he was to be with.

"What happened to him?" Rachel asked, thinking this was the right kind of question to be asking.

"He was found in his flat last night. A neighbour had popped over to wish him Happy Christmas and could hear the TV but couldn't get an answer. When he looked through the letter box, he glimpsed part of Mr McEwan's leg and he seemed to be lying on the living room floor." The police woman remained factual in her account. Her voice was monotone as the words tripped off her tongue as though she was reading a shopping list.

Rachel suddenly felt very sick.

"Are you ok Mrs Jenkins, you've gone very pale?" The male police officer spoke kindly to her.

"Yes, it's just a terrible shock. I can't believe no one would have checked on him for a whole year. It's so sad that another human can lie dead in a block of flats and no one knows." She placed her head in her hands and felt the bitter tears sting her eyes like little silvery needles of guilt.

"What did he die of?" Rachel added quickly, knowing that this was also a question that would be expected.

"It happens more often than you think Mrs Jenkins." Was the considered response from the policeman.

"You didn't check on him though did you Mrs Jenkins?" The accusatory tone was very apparent.

"No. No, I didn't. I wanted as little to do with him as possible. I had a very difficult marriage and a horrendous divorce so the fact that he hadn't been in touch was a relief." There was no point in Rachel's mind in hiding their torrid history, the police probably knew already anyway. Suki will have filled them in.

"Didn't his children wonder where he was?" Enquired the policewoman, who was busily writing copious notes in her official black notebook.

"They did ask, but I told them what I told you, I assumed he'd gone to Spain with Suki. He was forever letting the kids down, not turning up when he said he would, turning up late, leaving them waiting in the playground for hours after school. I decided not to encourage them to contact him because I felt they got upset and badly hurt every time he re-appeared in their lives." Rachel knew this would add fuel to their fire, but she felt sure they would have taken her to the station if they had suspected foul play.

"Ok, we'll be doing a postmortem on the body in between Christmas and New Year to determine the cause of death. You're not planning on leaving the country are you Mrs Jenkins?" The male police officer's tone changed dramatically and Rachel knew she was under suspicion.

"No. I've just had a baby, I'll be here with my family if you need me." She felt her cheeks redden and tried desperately to push the guilty feelings away.

"Ok, we'll be off. Sorry to have interrupted your Christmas Dinner. You can understand why we had to come round today though can't you Mrs Jenkins." This was a rhetorical question.

"Of course. It's ok, I understand. You've got a job to do. I don't know how I'm going to tell the kids on Christmas Day that their father is dead." The panic in her chest rose once again. She hadn't planned for this. Hurting her children was the last thing she wanted to do and now she was going to inflict pain on them when all she had wanted to do was to protect them from pain. She steadied herself on the radiator in the hallway as she saw the police officers walk down the driveway.

As Rachel closed and locked the front door she took a very deep breath in and exhaled her anxiety as best she could. It was now time to be the empathetic mother.

The Post Mortem

December 30th

Whether it was because Scarlett was the third child or whether it was that Rachel had her mind on other things didn't matter, the fact was, Scarlett behaved like a model baby for the next few days. Rachel was aware that whatever stress she felt, would be passed onto her newborn through her milk and her general mood. It was for these reasons, Rachel practiced her breathing, took herself off to her safe and comfortable bedroom and slept as much as she possibly could.

Christmas was a great distraction. There was plenty to be getting on with. After the shock of the visit from the police, Christmas dinner had been a muted affair.

There had been no easy way to tell Rosie and Sam that their father was dead. All the training in the world could not have prepared Rachel for the depth of pain she experienced as she conveyed the sad news to her beloved children.

She reassured herself that the momentary pain, they were experiencing now and would feel as they grieved for a man they barely knew anymore, would be nothing compared with the lifetime of heartache, disappointment and lies that they would be living through had he remained alive. Rachel knew in her heart that it wouldn't have been long before Alasdair was haranguing Rosie as much as he intimidated her. Rosie was blossoming into a beautiful and rebellious teenager, no longer the little girl that Alasdair had been able to manipulate so easily.

Rosie had already been questioning the need to spend time with her father, even before he disappeared. She had often resented having to visit him when there were sleepovers to go to and parties to attend. She had learned quickly that he would not make the effort to take her to such events, preferring instead to keep her at home with him and Sam. Rachel had begun to see the same signs of control over Rosie as Alasdair had applied to her and it had scared her.

There were indications that Rosie didn't want to spend time alone with her father, but nothing was ever said and despite Rachel's questioning, Rosie had never offered any information, sinister or otherwise. Rachel had put this reluctance down to being a pre-pubescent girl and resenting the intrusion of an interfering mother.

Rachel lay on her bed, feeding Scarlett for the fourth time that day. She'd emerged from her post-birth slumber and was very much into feeding throughout her waking hours. Rachel was exhausted, both emotionally and physically. The strain of not knowing what would happen to her was taking its toll on her internal state of mind and yet she could not say a word. The knot in her stomach was growing ever tighter and she was relieved to be able to sit alone frequently with her thoughts and her guzzling baby.

Radio Four was Rachel's constant companion during these quiet times. The melodic tones of the shipping forecast helped to distract Rachel. She sat wondering where Dogger and Fisher were and could guess that German Bite was somewhere in the North Sea, heading towards Germany. She liked to imagine little islands and outcrops in the dark sea with flagpoles stuck hard and fast into the solid ground of a formidable coastline, proudly displaying their shipping forecast name. One day, when this was all over and she was free, Rachel would learn about each name and discover where it was on the map.

Her thoughts were interrupted by the news. Another male abuser had got away with strangling his female partner, pouring bleach down her throat and hitting her over the head with a cricket bat. He'd received a suspended sentence because the judge felt the woman wasn't vulnerable enough. The male judge had stated in his sentencing statement that because the abused woman had a degree and some close friends, she could have escaped her abuser.

Rachel felt simultaneously deeply depressed and vindicated. She had a Master's Degree and quite a few friends, none of whom knew what she had been going through whilst she was with Alasdair. She had never been able to find the right words to describe what she had gone through with him. The furniture he threw always missed her, the words left no bruises on her body and the drinking was always behind closed doors. Most of their friends had assumed Rachel was the drinker because Alasdair always drove when they went out.

She was a successful business woman. Intelligent and to the outside world, very much in control of her own destiny and yet Alasdair had slowly eaten away her confidence over ten years and she had no idea how he had done it. She suspected keeping his secrets was part of the pattern of abuse. He'd forbidden her from talking to even her closest friend about his drinking, threatening her with vile language uttered close to her face with his teeth gritted in anger. She wiped her cheek as the memory of his spittle hitting her in the face as he spoke flashed across her mind. She had been too embarrassed to tell anyone about his bed wetting or that night after night he stayed up drinking until he was unconscious whilst she headed off to the marital bed alone. These weren't the types of things you discussed in polite company and they certainly weren't the type of thing an outwardly successful, intelligent woman told anyone. Rachel had convinced herself over the years that was she was experiencing was normal. She had hadn't a father at home so she had no idea how a husband ought to behave. She had no experience of alcoholism either and it had taken many years to realise what drove his mood swings and his vile verbal abuse.

As she listened to the radio, she felt as those these had all been excuses. Society didn't want to hear about smart women who were abused. Deep in her unconscious she knew the media would have twisted and turned her abuser's story so that she would have been portrayed as the career bitch who was so difficult to live with, her meek and mild house husband was driven to drink. Her own mother had suggested that to Rachel when she left Alasdair, "what did you do that drove him to drink?" Was her helpfully timed question. Her step-father had been on Alasdair's side too "I hope he takes you for every penny you have," had been his attitude when she left Alasdair.

A collective disbelief that a capable woman can be subject to abuse was the norm in Rachel's experience. No one believed her unless they had been abused themselves or had witnessed Alasdair's crazy behaviour. Eddie believed her when Alasdair changed the weekend arrangements whenever it suited him, especially when he discovered that Rachel and Eddie had a weekend away planned.

Rachel's best friend had believed her because she'd escaped an abusive marriage when she was only twenty-three. He'd been an alcoholic too, favouring curtain poles as his chosen weapon rather than cricket bats. The impact was equally painful.

Rachel sighed heavily as her tiny daughter pulled away from her breast and looked up into her face with that satiated expression babies have when they're full of milk. Rachel smiled a broad smile at this innocent little girl and promised she would do everything in her power to teach her to believe in herself, be confident and never put up with anyone controlling her in any way. Rachel understood more than ever that the way she educated her children was crucial to them all being able to steer well clear of the nutters who were out there waiting for the next victim.

The door-bell rang.

Rachel's heart stalled slightly as she fumbled with the catch on her feeding bra. She placed Scarlett carefully in her Moses Basket and kissed her on the cheek.

"Bye darling," she whispered, "Mummy's just going downstairs now, you play here. I'll be back. I promise." As she left the security of her bedroom, Rachel switched the baby monitor on and took the parent console downstairs with her.

The rest of the family were out at the park, taking the opportunity to get some fresh air whilst the weather was bright and clear. It was one of those beautiful crisp winter days which remind you there is still blue sky above the grey clouds of winter.

Rachel knew who this would be. She'd been expecting the knock at the door since Boxing Day.

"Good afternoon Mrs Jenkins" It was the same two police officers who had appeared on Christmas Day.

"Good afternoon." Rachel spoke clearly and confidently. "Please, come in."

"Thank you." The officers made a show of wiping their feet on the doormat. In Scotland it's polite to take your shoes off at the door when entering someone's home. This was something Rachel had always found quite quaint about living in Scotland. No such niceties were observed in Manchester.

"Can I get you a tea or coffee?" Rachel enquired.

"No. It's ok, we won't be staying long."

Rachel didn't know whether this was a good thing or not. She ushered the officers into the living room and closed the door, making sure she had the baby monitor next to her in case Scarlett cried.

"We'll get straight to the point." The female officer spoke first and took out her official notebook as she did so.

"The results of the post mortem on your ex-husband are back from the morgue." The officer paused, waiting for Rachel to speak.

"Ok," was the only thing Rachel could think of to say at that moment. Her mind was blank.

"It seems your ex-husband was a heavy drinker Mrs Jenkins." This was a statement as well as a question.

"Yes, yes, he was."

"Our pathologist seems to think he died of asphyxiation after a heavy session on the booze."

"Sorry, I don't understand." Rachel understood perfectly well what this meant, but she wanted to come across as stupid at this point in time.

"He choked on his own vomit whilst he was heavily inebriated Mrs Jenkins." The male officer, stepped in to helpfully explain the technicalities of Alasdair's cause of death.

"Oh. That's awful." Rachel put her hands up to her mouth and lowered her eyes.

"Yes. We believe he'd been prescribed Antabuse tablets by his GP and had been sober for at least six months. We think he'd stopped taking his tablets a day or two before and bought himself a large bottle of cheap vodka."

"He never could get through Christmas without a drink." Rachel commented, attempting to keep the sarcasm and bitterness out of her voice.

"We discovered he'd split up from his girlfriend the day before you saw him Mrs Jenkins and he had found the experience too difficult to cope with. We're assuming he stopped taking the Antabuse tablets so he could drink and bought himself the vodka before Christmas to make sure he had some in the flat and he intended to wait until the tablets had left his system. He didn't wait long enough it seems. Our pathologist told us that he was vomiting the lining of stomach up towards the end because the reaction to the alcohol was so violent. He also drank the vodka neat and we believe, drank it almost in one go."

"Could it have been a suicide attempt?" Offered Rachel.

"We're not sure. The Coroner will decide on that. It was our job to determine whether anyone else was involved in his death."

"Of course. Sorry." Rachel looked across at the officers. "And?"

"We are content that there was no foul play Mrs Jenkins." The female officer looked sharply at Rachel.

"I'm not sure whether that's a relief or just very, very sad." Rachel spoke her words with honesty. She was very sad. She was also relieved. Suki had ended their relationship and this had clearly been too much for Alasdair to bear. Both women had contributed to his death and yet neither were responsible. It had been Alasdair's decision to drink the vodka. In Rachel's eyes, its highly likely that he would have bought his own bottle had she not helpfully provided it.

The officers made their excuses and left the house.

Silence descended.

Rachel looked around her beautiful home with its designer fabrics, wooden floors and ever so modern kitchen with its Aga gleaming in the winter sunshine. She wandered through each room, touching the covers on her children's beds. Picking up their favourite toy here and there, and carefully placing it back to where it belonged.

She silently checked Scarlett and watched her as she slept soundly in her Moses Basket, blissfully unaware of anything except her own comfort.

How close had she come to being yet another victim of domestic violence, she will never know. What she did know was that she had protected her children from the horror of a father who was unpredictable. They would not be abducted or killed by him now. She'd saved them.

The front door swung open and three cold, but happy people noisily entered the house.

"We're back!" They all shouted together.

"I can hear that." Replied Rachel. "So am I." She muttered as she joyfully walked down the stairs. "So am I."

Printed in Great Britain
by Amazon